VALLEY OF DREAMS

When Kelly Taylor divorces her husband, she decides to make a new start with her ten-year-old son, Alex, in the tiny hamlet of Labadette, in rural France. Alex becomes increasingly close to Jean-Paul Borotra, a shepherd — and their closest neighbour. But there is tragedy surrounding Jean-Paul and, despite the attraction she feels, Kelly holds back from developing their friendship further. And then, when Alex goes to visit his father in London, events take a frightening turn . . .

Books by June Gadsby
in the Linford Romance Library:

PRECIOUS LOVE
KISS TODAY GOODBYE
SECRET OBSESSIONS
THE ROSE CAROUSEL
THE SAFE HEART
THE MIRACLE OF LOVE

JUNE GADSBY

---◆---

VALLEY OF DREAMS

Complete and Unabridged

LINFORD
Leicester

First published in Great Britain in 2006

First Linford Edition
published 2007

British Library CIP Data

Gadsby, June
    Valley of dreams.—Large print ed.—
Linford romance library
1. Divorced women—Fiction
2. Love stories
3. Large type books
I. Title
823.9′2 [F]

ISBN 978–1–84617–642–5

Published by
F. A. Thorpe (Publishing)
Anstey, Leicestershire

Set by Words & Graphics Ltd.
Anstey, Leicestershire
Printed and bound in Great Britain by
T. J. International Ltd., Padstow, Cornwall

This book is printed on acid-free paper

First Encounter

Kelly Taylor knew it was going to be a difficult day the moment she opened her eyes and saw the rain. This was southwest France, for goodness' sake! It hardly ever rained. Not in May. But it *was* raining, coming down in liquid glass sheets, blurring the countryside and turning it into a soggy watercolour painting.

'A bit like my life,' she muttered into the steamed-up window-pane of her bedroom window. 'Soggy, with shades of grey.'

Actually the soggy bit, where she had wept buckets for days on end, had dried into a heavy brick in the pit of her stomach. But at least there were no more real tears. A touch of moisture coating the eyeballs, that was all.

'Well, I'm blowed if I'm going to live forever feeling like this!' she muttered to herself as she put some vigour into getting the day started.

'Hey, Mum, what's all the noise?'

Alex, still in pyjamas and rubbing his eyes, came blindly down the ladder from his attic bedroom. He missed the bottom two rungs and fell in a heap at Kelly's feet.

'Ouch!'

'Alex Taylor, how many times have I told you about being more careful!' she scolded mildly, hauling him to his feet. He peered about him short-sightedly. 'Go on! Off to the bathroom and make sure you use *hot* water this time — and *soap*.'

Her son grinned cheekily at her and she aimed a playful slap at him, but he ducked out of her reach and ran off to the bathroom. He only bumped into one packing crate on the way, which was amazing since he wasn't wearing his glasses.

Kelly stared at the collection of boxes stacked in the middle of the living-room and sighed. Her life was packed

2

into a few pieces of cardboard. It didn't look a lot for thirty-two years.

Peter, of course, had taken more than this back to England with him. Well, that other woman was welcome to his clutter; his books on science, his collections of miniature cars and train sets that nobody was allowed to touch, not even Alex.

At least he had left her their son. Alex had shown no inclination to go with his father. She had asked him over and over again, just to be sure.

'Mum!' He had fixed her with exasperated eyes that looked huge through his thick lenses. 'I'm staying with you!'

Sometimes talking to Alex was like talking to an adult. She tended to forget he was only ten, because he often seemed more mature than she was.

They ate a silent breakfast, sitting companionably together on the front step under the roof overhang, watching the rain. The deafening sound of its constant drumming was challenged only by the crunch of Alex's cornflakes as he ate. Kelly wrapped her hands around her cup of coffee and stared ahead into nothing.

As she drained her cup she glanced at her watch. 'Time to start moving,' she said.

Back in the living-room, she stretched brown sticky tape across the top of the last box, reached for the scissors from the mantelpiece, and saw the mirror. 'Darn! I forgot you!'

Her reflection stared back, all fluffy auburn hair and wide blue eyes. Like a little girl lost, she thought with a grimace, then reprimanded herself for that flash of self-pity. After all, there was a new life waiting to get started. She was determined not to be miserable.

Kelly had been determined about a few things recently. Like asking Peter for a divorce. It had taken the wind out of her sails when he had got it in first. She hadn't been totally surprised, though, when she had got over the shock and started to think about it. Life in rural France hadn't worked for him. He missed the hustle and bustle of big industrial towns and the stress of holding down a responsible job with a decent salary that paid a mortgage and allowed a new car every year.

Out here, in France, they had planned to live 'the good life', living off the land, being self-sufficient. It had taken Peter six months to realise that 'the good life' only worked when somebody else was writing the script and doing the work.

She ought to have suspected something when he was away for longer and longer periods in England, encouraging her to stay on in France. Not that it took much encouragement. She loved it here.

'Mirror, mirror, on the wall!' Alex chanted from the open doorway and she spun around to find him leaning against the doorpost, his head to one side, regarding her. 'Has it told you yet, Mum, that you're the most beautiful of all?'

'Fu-*nny!*' She grinned at him. 'I do *not* talk to mirrors.'

'That's a relief. I thought maybe you'd gone flaky on me.'

She frowned and glanced back at the mirror, remembering how Peter in all his vanity used to preen before it, yet he had always been ready to tell her about *her* shortcomings. Bust not big enough, hips too wide, ankles too thick, tongue too sharp . . .

'I forgot to pack it,' she said, frowning again at the mirror. 'Oh, well. Maybe it can be our present to the next owners. I never did like the thing anyway.'

The decision to sell the house, which was already in her name, had been taken the day Peter had left for the last time.

'Do what you want with the place,' he had said. 'I have my flat in London. And, of course, Maggie has her own home in Dorset.'

Maggie! The other woman. The *older* other woman. Most husbands ran off

6

with younger women. Not Peter. He liked mature, motherly types.

Kelly, feeling restless, had driven out into the mountains. She had been parked on a hillside overlooking a pretty valley and five minutes later she had been making a note of an ancient farmhouse sporting a sign that said '*A vendre*' — 'For Sale'. It had appealed to her, nestling in its chocolate box beauty with the mellow evening sun melting all over it like molten gold.

She had bought it the next day. Sheer madness, of course, but there had been something so magical about the valley and the house and . . .

Kelly rubbed at the hairs rising on the back of her neck and gave an involuntary shudder. She had a feeling about this new home of hers. It was right for her.

'I hope I'm going to like this place,' Alex said as she ushered him towards the car that was packed to bursting with their more immediate needs. The rest of the boxes and a few pieces of remaining furniture were to follow by van two days later.

'Well, Alex, there are times in life when it's good to take a risk or two.' She smiled at him confidently, trying to ignore the slow stirring of butterflies that suddenly felt more like apprehension than excitement.

'Just as long as you remember that it was *your* idea.' Alex's face twisted to one side and he stuck a finger behind his glasses and rubbed an eye. 'Whatever happens, I don't want to get blamed for it.'

'Do I ever blame you for anything?'

'You blamed me for Monsieur Lemaitre's chickens!'

'Yes, well, you shouldn't have left that gate open and Zoltan wouldn't have chased them.'

Suddenly there was a scuffling noise from behind Kelly's seat and a cold, wet black nose nudged her elbow.

She turned round and gaped in amazement at the dog.

'Zoltan? Alex! What's he doing here?'

Alex cowered slightly in his seat. 'Er — dunno. He must have sneaked in when I wasn't looking.'

'And I suppose he packed himself in tight and covered himself with my best anorak! Oh, Alex! You know we can't take him. He doesn't belong to us. It would be stealing.'

Alex's face puckered and he stared down at his hands. He and Zoltan had been great pals for three years. The separation was going to be hard and Kelly felt bad about it. If only Peter had allowed Alex to have a dog of his own the problem wouldn't have arisen, but Peter was no animal lover.

'Come on, love, be reasonable.' Kelly put an arm about her son and gave him a tight hug. 'Look, when we get settled in our new home we'll think about getting a dog. Two, if it'll make you happy.'

With a loud sniff, Alex slid out of the car and pulled at Zoltan's collar until the dog squeezed out with a reluctant yelp.

Kelly watched, her throat tightening, as boy and dog went through their last farewell. Alex finally gave Zoltan a sharp order to return home. The dog trotted reluctantly away, tail between its legs, stopping from time to time to glance hopefully over its shoulder, pink tongue lolling and rain glistening on its thick coat.

'Did you mean that, Mum?' Alex said as he got back into the car, his voice all wobbly with emotion. 'About the dog, I mean. Is it a promise?'

'Yes, sweetheart. It's a promise.'

* * *

The rain continued steadily, but finally petered out to a fine drizzle by the time they stopped for lunch just outside Pau. Kelly ate sparingly while Alex tucked in to his beef and bean stew, cleaning his plate with chunks of country bread like a traditional Frenchman, talking volubly all the while.

'It's a good job your father can't see

you now.' Kelly laughed. 'He'd be appalled at your table manners.'

'Monsieur Lacoste wipes his plate clean with his bread and he's the mayor,' Alex said, as if that excused everything.

'Just remember that it may be all right for downtown France, but it could be frowned upon in England. Especially at your grandmother's table.'

Alex rolled his eyes dramatically, recalling maturing experiences at the hands of his paternal grandmother. Then he brightened. 'But now that you and Dad are getting a divorce I won't need to see her again, will I?'

'An occasional visit will be necessary, Alex. She is still your grandmother, after all.'

'Oh.' It was said with a certain amount of disappointment.

Kelly's parents were both dead. They had only lived to see Alex reach his second birthday, so he really didn't remember them, which was a pity. Unlike Harriet Taylor they would have been proud of their plucky grandson who was small for his age and looked as fragile as fine porcelain. His appearance, however, was deceiving. Alex was a bundle of energy and what he lacked in stature he made up for with a strong personality.

'As soon as possible, Alex, we must see about school. I think I saw one in the village. It won't be for long, then next year you'll be going to the *lycée*. No doubt they'll have one in a nearby town.'

'There aren't any nearby towns,' Alex said with authority. 'I looked at the map. There's nothing but mountains for miles.'

She smiled and picked a thread from his sweatshirt. 'We'll see.'

'I don't mind. I can stay at home and help you. We can breed dogs — those big Pyrenean dogs. The white ones that look like polar bears.'

'Oh no, young man. Your education comes first, no matter what.'

Then they were back on the road

again, with Alex navigating, following the route through Arudy where they stopped to buy provisions for the next few days. As they entered the Ossau Valley through a thick swathe of forest, the sun struggled through and pockets of mist began to rise and spread out over the landscape.

The roads were narrow and winding and once they started to climb toward the Col du Pourtalet Kelly needed to keep all her attention on the road ahead. She wasn't used to driving in these conditions and it was a bit nerve-wracking, especially when meeting on-coming vehicles, mostly Land-Rovers and jeeps driven by farmers, and the odd tourist or two.

'I think this is it.' Kelly parked the car on a rise and let out a long sigh of relief. Just to stop driving was bliss.

Alex, already out of the car, was standing on a rock looking out over the valley before them. 'There's nothing here!'

'Don't be silly, Alex.' She got out and joined him.

He was right. There was nothing there.

'But I'm sure this is the valley. The village — it was right there — a bit over to the left and . . . '

There was nothing to see but swirling, milky mist as if one of the great, grey-white clouds had tumbled from the sky and was blanketing the whole valley. She could even taste it, that strange, sooty residue that clung to the tongue.

'It was here, I know it was,' Kelly insisted. 'A tiny little hamlet called Labadette. It looked like it hadn't changed for hundreds of years.'

'Maybe it disappeared, like the place in that old film you used to like.'

Kelly gave him a quick look. 'What? Brigadoon, do you mean? Well, yes, it did look a bit like that. Maybe that's why I fell in love with it.'

She dreaded the thought of having to backtrack and search for the right road. The journey had been horrendous enough up to this point, what with the rain and the fog and roads that were so narrow, dropping off to nothing at the edge.

'There's a telegraph pole,' Alex pointed, and then they both stiffened as their ears picked up a muffled but distinctive sound that got closer and closer. 'What's that? It sounds like Santa Claus on his sleigh.'

It certainly did sound like bells, and lots of them. It was as if the valley was singing.

Then, suddenly, something moved through the mist fifty yards ahead. A dark shape materialised as the bells got louder and the tinkling grew more strident, like the clanging of discordant church bells.

The shape took on human form. In the background now they could hear the bleating of sheep and the echoing bark of a dog. The shepherd stopped, turned and whistled a series of signalling notes. Then he was walking again, striding out purposefully, coming towards them where they stood on the crest of the hill.

Kelly saw a broad, strong face looking up at her from beneath a large, flat black beret. From that distance his eyes appeared to be dark and brooding. Beneath the lightweight waterproof poncho, which he had thrown back off his shoulders, he wore a *gilet* of lambskin, and brown corduroy pants that were well worn into a comfortable, shapeless item of clothing.

'*Bonjour!*' she called out and took a step forward to meet him.

The shepherd nodded, bellowed out a sharp word of command to his dog, then turned sherry brown eyes on Kelly and smiled. The smile ended in deep creases around his eyes. He was tanned and weathered, but he wasn't old. Certainly no more than forty, she guessed. It was difficult to tell in the diffused light and the fact that he had on him a day or two's dark growth of beard.

'Are you lost?' he asked. His accent was unfamiliar, sounding almost Spanish.

16

Kelly gave him a rueful smile. 'Perhaps. I'm looking for a village called Labadette. I thought it was in this valley, but I don't see it, so perhaps I was mistaken.'

'*Non, madame*, you are not mistaken.' He turned and waved an arm behind him. 'You follow this road. Go straight ahead. It is there in the mist.'

'Oh, thank goodness!'

'But I ask you one thing, *madame*. Wait a few moments, *hein*?'

'Why's that?'

Kelly followed his gaze and saw the reason for his request. The road was filled with a large flock of sheep plodding up the hill towards them, emerging out of the mist like cotton wool balls on legs, black faces nodding, bells jangling.

Kelly laughed. 'I see what you mean.'

The shepherd gave a shrill whistle and a big white Pyrenean dog came bounding up to him, dancing around his legs.

'Come, Tricot!' The man turned,

nodding again, dark eyes curious on her face.

'Aw, Mum, isn't he super?' Alex enthused, already down on his knees and fondling the dog's furry ears.

'Alex! Be careful! Mountain dogs can be dangerous!'

'Your mother is right, young man. Never approach a strange dog without first being sure that he is friendly.'

'But he *is* friendly,' Alex argued, as his face was washed by a large pink tongue.

The man grinned down at him and nodded. 'Yes, Tricot is a good dog. The best. He knows by instinct you will not harm him or his sheep — or his master!'

He nodded again at Kelly and moved on. The dog hesitated, anxious to make friends, but at a further whistle from the shepherd he shot obediently off. The sheep followed, tightly bunched together, bumping and nudging. There were at least two hundred of them, no doubt being moved up to the high pastures to wait for the thaw in July, when they would go even higher yet up the mountain. The 'transhumance' they called it. In October they would be brought back down to wintering pens.

'Oh, Mum, wasn't he gorgeous?' Alex was still staring longingly up the road.

'Well, he wasn't the most handsome man in the world, but . . . ' Kelly answered without thinking and, when Alex grinned, she flushed. 'Oh, you mean the dog! Yes, lovely.'

'And the shepherd wasn't bad either, was he?'

'Get in the car, Alex, before one of these sheep takes a bite out of your backside! You cheeky imp!'

They sat in the car patiently waiting for the flock to clear the road. Kelly pretended not to notice Alex's sudden high spirits and the fact that he kept looking at her sideways and sniggering into his sweatshirt. Really, he was so sharp he would cut himself one of these days, she thought fondly.

Their New Home

The mist lifted as they drove down into the valley, and there before them was the quaint, unspoiled village of Labadette.

'Wow! It's old!' Alex crowed as Kelly parked the car in front of the café. 'It's got to be the oldest place in the world!'

Kelly laughed, got out of the car and stretched luxuriously in the warm sunshine. 'Well, not quite. I think there are still a few places existing that are older than this one.'

'*Merde!*'

They jumped at the sound of the coarse female voice. There was a loud rattle of bottles, a crash of glass, and then a squawking chicken, wings flapping frantically, landed right in front of them. A stern-faced woman in apron and muddy rubber boots came around the corner of the building and pulled up short in front of them.

'*Bonjour, madame!*' Kelly walked towards the woman, smiling, then saw the long-bladed knife smeared with blood in her hand and took a hasty step back.

'What do you want, *madame?* Are you lost?'

'No — no, I'm not lost. I've come to — um — to live in Labadette.'

The woman's eyes widened perceptibly, then she looked down at the knife she was clutching and made an impatient noise. 'I am killing the chickens. It is my husband's job, but he is too lazy. He looks at the television in the middle of the day. You want coffee?'

'That would be — um — very nice, thank you.'

Kelly looked towards the café. In the doorway, a portly man rocked gently on the balls of his feet as he regarded her benevolently, a grubby tea towel stretched across his bulging paunch.

'*Madame!*' He inclined his head in her direction and smoothed his big black brush moustache.

'*Bonjour, monsieur.*' Kelly pulled Alex forward. 'I'm Madame Taylor and this is my son, Alexander. We've bought the house . . . '

The man stepped forward and grabbed her hand, pumping it up and down and beaming at her jovially. She winced, but managed to keep smiling.

'You are most welcome, *madame.*' He flapped pudgy fingers in the direction of the woman. 'She is my wife. Take no notice of her. She is angry. She is *always* angry.'

'Why?' Alex asked and received a sharp nudge from his mother.

'*Bauf!* She doesn't like this, she doesn't like that. I cannot please her. She offered you coffee?'

'Yes, she did, but . . . '

'The coffee is awful. I offer you a glass of red wine — yes?'

'Well . . . '

'Come! Come into the café. I am pleased to serve you.'

'It's very kind, but . . . '

'Sit down. Here. Young man, what is your pleasure?'

'Can I have a *panaché*, please?' he said, requesting a shandy.

'No, you cannot, Alex Taylor.' Kelly raised her eyebrows at her son, then turned to the man. 'He'll have a lemonade, monsieur, and thank you.'

The man — Monsieur Armand Soubirous, or so it said above the door — passed Alex a can of juice, and poured two generous glasses of red wine, one of which he placed before Kelly.

'*À la votre!*' He saluted her with his glass.

Kelly sipped at her wine, which tasted more like stale vinegar.

'Very nice,' she said, trying not to grimace.

'Can I have a taste?' Alex helped himself before she could stop him and he was much more spontaneous in his response. 'Aargh! Puke!'

'Alex, drink your lemonade and let's go,' Kelly warned him in rapid English as she smiled apologetically at Monsieur Soubirous.

'So! You are going to live in the old Borotra place, *hein?* There is much work to be done. Your husband — he is a good *bricoleur?'*

The idea of Peter ever wielding a saw or a hammer in some DIY made her smile. If you showed him a loose screw he used to run a mile.

'I don't have a husband, monsieur,' she said and saw his eyebrows disappear into his sparse hairline.

'Ah!' he exclaimed.

Madame Soubirous came in carrying a large zinc tub and she was spattered all over with blood. Alex stared at her in horror and his lemonade missed his mouth and ran down his chin. Kelly didn't like to look inside the tub, but she was pretty sure it would be full of headless chickens heading for *la soupe.*

'Here!' the woman thrust the tub at her husband. 'Put this in the kitchen.'

'Oui, ma biche!' he said good-naturedly and got a growl for his pains.

He indicated Kelly with a jerk of his big head. 'Madame doesn't have a husband, Delphine.'

Madame Soubirous' eyes swivelled round and narrowed as she looked at Kelly. 'You are a widow?'

Kelly shook her head.

'Divorced, *alors!*' Monsieur Soubirous suggested in some horror.

'Yes — well, not exactly . . . ' Kelly stuttered and gave Alex a meaningful push towards the door. 'Thank you so much for the wine. Oh, I believe you are holding the key to my house?'

Delphine Soubirous wiped her hands down her front and fumbled about behind the bar counter, muttering to herself all the while, then produced a large, gothic-looking key which she held out.

'Thank you.' Kelly reached out and grasped the key, but the woman hung on to it, her eyes narrowing even more.

'There are things you should know about the Borotra house,' she said.

25

'Delphine!' Her husband's voice held a warning. 'This is not the moment. Be nice. It is not the Englishwoman's fault that she has bought the house. Take your anger out on Jean-Paul.'

'Bah!' The woman released the key and threw one hand up in the air.

Kelly took the key, thanked them both again and hurried Alex out to the car where a group of curious children and some mangy-looking dogs were gathered.

'What did she mean, Mum?' Alex asked, eyeing the dogs longingly.

'Heaven knows! We're in the French countryside, Alex. People are a little eccentric.'

Alex jumped into the car beside her. The mist had completely cleared, and now the sun was hot and dazzling through the windscreen.

'What mountain's that?' he wanted to know, pointing at a distant snow-covered pyramid.

'That's the Pic du Midi d'Ossau,' Kelly told him. 'There's an observatory on the top, I believe. We'll have to visit it one day.'

Alex nodded enthusiastically, taking in the rolling foothills, the scattered clumps of trees and forests and sparkling streams. 'It's super, Mum. A lot better than living in a town.'

'I hope so, Alex.' She also hoped that not all the villagers would be like Madame Soubirous.

★ ★ ★

The house looked bigger and more ramshackle than it had the day she had first seen it. As Kelly put the key in the lock she experienced a few misgivings. What if it all was a big mistake?

OK, so she may have been a fool to act so irresponsibly, but at the time she had felt the need to do something crazy and out of character. Peter had kept her on too tight a rein for too long. He, of course, never did anything without working out every last detail first.

The heavy door swung back with a

slight creak and the sunlight filtered into the hall in a curtain of dust-filled light. The atmosphere was laden with the mustiness of two hundred years of living, and stale polish.

'Ugh!' Alex grunted and rubbed at his nose with the flat of his hand.

'Don't worry,' she told him. 'The smell will go once we can open all the doors and windows and get some air through the place.'

The agent had told her the house had been empty and unlived in for some years, though it was well maintained and was still connected to all the services.

Somebody had certainly done some work here recently. The hall had been painted. You could still smell the fresh paint.

The room on the left had been redecorated, too. It was a typical French country house living-room, spacious with a long, solid oak dining-table in the centre. An old settee sat before a huge open fireplace. It was fairly worn and looked uncomfortable, but it would do until she could replace it.

The kitchen on the other side of the hall was large and basic, the walls hung with well-used copper pans, and there was an open cooking range that probably helped to heat the whole house.

Opening off it, a smaller scullery was even more basic, the shelves still stocked with ancient preserves, bottled fruits and vegetables. She would need to contact the previous owner about that.

There was another room at the back, north facing, that was completely empty apart from a few rusting garden tools. With the introduction of a long picture window it would make an excellent studio, Kelly decided, already planning for the future. She could start painting again, take up where she had left off when she'd got married.

'Hey, Mum!' Alex's voice reached her from somewhere above. 'There's a fantastic view from up here.'

She climbed the stairs, thankful that they were in a good, solid state of repair.

Upstairs, there were four reasonably big bedrooms. The biggest had an *en suite* bathroom and on the other side there was a separate shower unit and WC.

Outside, a balcony ran along all four sides of the house and everywhere she looked the views were spectacular.

'Isn't it just mega-cool?' Alex was running around the balcony, his excitement overflowing.

Kelly laughed and looked out towards the distant blue-glazed mountains with their attendant green foothills. She couldn't wait to get out there and start exploring. The place would be abundant with wild flowers at this time of year.

As she gazed up at the higher slopes rising from the meadowland behind the house, something caught her eye. A flash of brown and creamy white.

'Did you see that?' Alex was beside her, pointing. 'What was it? A deer?'

'I'm not sure — oh, look!' As she spoke an izard broke cover, dashed across the hillside and jumped up on to a stack of rocks before blending into the mountain décor.

'A goat!' Alex cried in excitement, looking up at her, his eyes shining.

'An izard, Alex — a Pyrenean ibex. They're very like the *chamois* of the Alps.'

'Will there be any marmots around here?'

Kelly laughed. Alex had a passion for marmots since being allowed to feed some in an animal park when he was very young. He even had a collection of the stuffed toy variety, some of which gave strident wolf whistles when you walked past them.

'I'm sure there'll be lots of them in these hills. We'll hear them whistling.'

'Like that, do you mean?'

In the distance a series of whistles travelled across the valley, then there was an answering call from the other side.

'I think you'll find those whistles are man-made,' she said, remembering the whistling of the shepherd they had met earlier. In the old days the shepherds of the Pyrenees had devised their own special language, using a set series of whistles. It was their only method of communicating with one another when huge distances apart. Like many other old traditions, whistling was dying out, like the shepherds themselves.

'Who do you think lives in that cottage up there?' Alex was short-sighted, but he rarely missed anything.

The tiny cottage, half-hidden among trees, was hardly more than a cabin and was probably somebody's holiday home.

'Maybe nobody lives there,' Kelly said, shading her eyes against the early evening sun. 'Anyway, we'll find out soon. They'll have to pass our house to get to the road.'

Alex had found his binoculars and was having a better look at the cottage.

'They've got a dog!' he cried out blissfully. 'There's a kennel — a big one.'

Kelly smiled and left him scouring the hillsides looking for more izards and marmots.

She decided to take the largest of the four bedrooms for herself. It was light and airy and had a fantastic view. She couldn't imagine a nicer sight to wake up to every morning. There was an old double bed with sagging, jangling springs and an ancient mattress that she suspected was filled with straw. Well, it would have to do until her own furniture arrived.

She didn't feel much like struggling with the stove in the kitchen, so they made do with gigantic French stick sandwiches of rich, dark red sausage and chunks of cheese. It pleased Alex to be so casual.

They sat on the terrace at the back of the house and watched the sun turn crimson, listening to the birds as they flitted swiftly to and fro, frenetic in their last-minute daily routine.

They were munching away happily when they heard another kind of whistling. Not signals this time, but a happy, carefree tune as someone came up the track from the village.

Both Kelly and Alex leaned forward, eager to meet their first visitor. Kelly recognised at once the black beret and the broad shoulders of the shepherd as he plodded wearily towards them up the hill.

Alex was already bouncing down the track to meet man and dog — especially the dog, which gave a welcoming bark and allowed the boy to run small pale hands through its thick fur.

'*Bon soir!*' Kelly called out to the shepherd. 'We met earlier today.'

'Yes, I remember.' He turned to watch Alex who was trying to persuade the dog to play, but the animal, though friendly, simply watched the stick being thrown with a laconic air.

'Doesn't he know how to fetch, *monsieur?*' Alex couldn't hide his frustration.

The shepherd swept his beret from his head, revealing a thick thatch of dark brown hair that gleamed in the light of the setting sun. He wore it long and tied back in a ponytail. What surprised Kelly was the fact that she found it rather attractive.

'Tricot is a working dog,' the man said, mopping his broad forehead and replacing his beret. 'He does not normally have time to play. Right now, he is tired. We are both tired after a long day with the sheep.'

'Oh, I see.' Disappointment shadowed Alex's face. He'd obviously been hoping for a new friend to replace Zoltan.

'Alex is crazy about animals,' Kelly said. 'We're going to look for a dog for him as soon as possible.'

Again the slow, solemn nod, then the man turned to look at her and the fire of the sun was reflected in his eyes, bringing them vibrantly alive.

'A boy needs a dog, always. I will look out for one for him.'

'That's very kind of you.' Kelly stepped down from the terrace and went towards him, hand outstretched.

'I'm Kelly Taylor, by the way. We've just moved in.'

There was a slight lift of his square chin. His eyes flickered over her, went to the house and then returned. He grasped her hand firmly. His skin was warm and dry and slightly roughened by the hard manual labour of his job.

'Yes, I know.'

Kelly laughed lightly. 'I suppose news travels fast in a small village. Do you live here?'

'Yes.' He nodded towards the cottage on the hill. 'Up there.'

'Alex will be pleased to have Tricot as a neighbour. I don't suppose you know the people who owned this house, do you? I need to contact them to talk about the things they've left behind.'

'As a matter of fact, I know the owner very well.'

'Oh, good! What's his name? Does he still live in the area?'

'His name is Jean-Paul Borotra and — yes, he still lives here.'

'Good. Where can I find him?'

'You are looking at him, *madame*.'

Kelly stared at him, slightly embarrassed and more than a little interested. She didn't know why she should be either.

In the meadow, Alex, intent on demonstrating how dogs were expected to play, was down on all fours, a small tree branch clenched between his teeth. The big Pyrenean dog was lying in the grass a few feet away, panting and yawning widely.

'At least I don't have to try to find you, *monsieur*,' she said and wished he wouldn't look at her quite so intently with those penetrating eyes of his. 'The agent told me that the house was being sold with everything intact, but there are quite a few things I'd like to ask you about. I'm sure you didn't mean to leave so much.'

'I took everything I wanted. The house belonged to my grandparents. I haven't lived in it for many years. The cottage is sufficient for my needs.'

'You're not married, then?'

Kelly could have kicked herself for sounding so curious because he gave her a strange look that bordered on the apprehensive.

'I mean — the cottage looks too small for more than one person,' she added, flustered.

'No, *madame*, I am not married. It is not easy to be a good shepherd and at the same time a good husband . . . ' He glanced over at Alex. ' . . . or a good father.'

'No, I can imagine it's a difficult life.'

He smiled briefly and his head tilted to one side. 'I take it you met Armand and Delphine Soubirous this afternoon?'

'Yes. Monsieur Soubirous was very kind. He gave me a glass of wine.'

'Ha! That poison he sells in the bar? It is the wine of his brother, Pierre, who works in the holiday village of Gourette. He is a chef. His cooking is infinitely better than his wine-making, I assure you.'

'Well, it was a nice gesture anyway,'

Kelly said and saw his dark brows descend into a frown.

'And Delphine? How was she?'

Kelly gave a wry smile. 'I think I caught her at a bad time.'

'She wasn't very friendly?' It was a rhetorical question.

'Not very. Perhaps she doesn't approve of foreigners.'

The shepherd threw back his head and laughed, showing a row of strong, square white teeth.

'It would not matter to Delphine what nationality you are,' he confided. 'What does upset her is the fact that you are a woman.'

Kelly stared at him and drew in a deep breath. 'Well, she has nothing to fear from me. Her husband is quite safe.'

Jean-Paul Borotra put his hands on his hips and smiled wryly. 'Armand is not the object of her anxiety, *madame*.'

'Really?'

He looked at her some more, then, without explaining further, he turned his attention to Alex. 'Will the boy be going to school in the village?'

'I suppose so, yes — for a short while, until he's ready to go to the *lycee*. He'll be eleven in September.'

'He is small for his age. I took him to be much younger.'

Kelly looked lovingly at her son. 'He is small,' she agreed, nodding, 'but he's quite strong, and very intelligent. That much he gets from his father, so I'm grateful.'

'Ah!' It was amazing how much could be conveyed by that one small sound. By uttering it, the Frenchman gave the impression that he knew everything there was to be known about her.

'Is it a good school?' she asked. 'It looks very small.'

'It has twenty-three pupils and one excellent school-mistress, Yvette Bernardi. I will tell her to call on you.'

'That would be very useful, thank you.'

'It is my pleasure. We are neighbours, *non*?'

They were neighbours, yes, Kelly thought, and wondered what the shepherd did to pass the time in his lonely cottage. Even a shepherd must have some time when he is not working. With only a dog to talk to, it must be a pretty isolated life.

Jean-Paul Borotra wished her a *bonne soirée*. He had a nice smile, Kelly thought as she watched him go, and was so distracted with curious thoughts of him that she didn't notice how cold the evening had turned.

To The Rescue

The next day was Sunday, but Kelly had no intention of making it a day of rest. Her furniture was arriving tomorrow and there were things to do. First, she had to figure out how the stove worked in the kitchen. They needed heating. She had shivered convulsively last night, even though the day had been extremely warm.

By the time she was up and dressed, having showered in ice-cold water, Alex was already on the balcony with his binoculars, enthusing over what he could see. At least that was one present from his father that had been the perfect choice for their nature-loving son.

'Aw! Mum, come and see this!'

She went out to him, pulling him back from the rather rickety railing that went around the balcony. He had been leaning over it perilously and the old, worn rails didn't look too safe. That, she thought, making a mental note, would be the first job to have done.

Alex handed her the binoculars and pointed up into the sky where a group of three big birds of prey were circling, already soaring on the thermals as the warming sun beat down on the land.

'Do you know what they are?' she asked, testing his knowledge as she kept the glasses on the birds.

'Condors!' he shouted, then giggled. He always liked to pull her leg. 'OK, OK. They're Griffin Vultures — yes?'

'Two of them are, yes,' she confirmed, handing the glasses back to him. 'The third is a buzzard. Well done. Now, come and have some breakfast and let's get the day started.'

The stove defeated her. Twice she got it lit and twice it flickered for a few minutes and died.

'Maybe it needs cleaning out,' Alex suggested, being helpful.

'Right,' Kelly said, rolling up her

shirtsleeves and getting down on her knees in front of the stove.

It was certainly very dirty inside, caked with soot and tarry grime.

Outside, she could hear the church bell chiming out across the valley, and the distant jingling of sheep and cattle bells. There was something so tranquil and soothing about the sounds, together with the constant chorus from the birds and the occasional burst from the crickets and the frogs.

Neither of them heard the approach of footsteps up the track and along the path to their open front door. Kelly was just wiping a sooty hand across her face and muttering softly to herself over her inability to get any joy out of the stove when a voice behind her made her jump.

'Madame Taylor — bonjour!'

The woman standing there was tall and slim, around thirty-five, and pretty in a natural sort of way with her light, golden brown hair worn in a long plait down her back. She was deeply tanned and looked as if she enjoyed the sun.

'Hello, can I help you?' Kelly said, scrambling to her feet self-consciously. In her haste she spoke in English.

The woman just looked at her, smiling, her eyes flitting about the kitchen curiously. 'I knocked, but you did not hear me,' she stated flatly. 'Jean-Paul tells me that you would like your son to attend school in the village.'

Kelly frowned, then remembered how the shepherd had mentioned the school-teacher during their brief conversation last night.

'Oh! You are . . . ?'

'Yvette Bernardi.'

'Do sit down, Madame Bernardi . . . ' Kelly said, thinking she must look a terrible mess and, at the same time, thinking that the shepherd had lost no time in contacting the teacher.

'It is *mademoiselle*, but please, call me Yvette. This is your son?'

'*Bonjour, mademoiselle*. My name is Alex.' Alex stuck his hand out and beamed when the woman clasped it momentarily and gave him a special smile as she stooped to kiss his cheeks.

'I would offer you a cup of coffee,' Kelly said apologetically, 'but I can't get the stove to work and my electric kettle hasn't arrived yet.'

'I never drink coffee, thank you.' A pair of cool grey eyes fixed themselves on Kelly's face. 'If you need help with the stove you must ask at the café. Armand knows all the artisans around here.'

'I'll do that — thank you.'

'You are here for the summer?'

Kelly shook her head. 'No, we plan to live here, Alex and I.'

The woman's eyes were wandering again. 'I see. It is unusual, a woman on her own, coming to such an isolated spot. How will you survive, Madame Taylor, without a husband to support you?'

Kelly was tempted to ask the school-teacher how *she* survived without a husband, but she put a tight lid on her sudden flare of irritation.

'I'm an artist. I illustrate children's books — or, at least, I used to before I got married.'

'Ah!'

There was that sound again. Kelly didn't know why she should feel so irritated. She didn't like the woman's attitude. There was something about it that seemed directed personally at her. A little like the woman at the café.

'I think this is a perfect setting for an artist to work in, don't you?' she said quickly and the cool grey eyes were upon her again, narrowed and hooded.

Yvette Bernardi gave a small shrug. She looked down at Alex with a sigh. 'Perhaps Alex would like to report to me tomorrow morning. We can take care of the official enrolment later on. I suppose you have registered with *monsieur le maire*?' she asked, mentioning the mayor.

'Not yet. Everything happened so quickly. Who is the *maire* of Labadette? I didn't notice a *mairie*. Is there one?'

'But of course. It is in the back room

of the café. Monsieur Soubirous is our *maire*. Madame Soubirous is my aunt.'

'Am I the only foreigner in Labadette?' Kelly asked.

The school-teacher shook her head. 'No. There is Jean-Paul Borotra.'

Kelly blinked her surprise. 'The shepherd? But he's French, surely?' she protested.

'Yes — but he is a Basque. *Au revoir, madame.*'

'She's super!' Alex enthused as the school-teacher's tall, willowy figure made its way slowly back down the track towards the village.

'Hmm,' was all Kelly could say, wondering why she didn't like the Frenchwoman. Maybe it was that slightly fragile look, the fey, little-girl voice, and the hint of something secret.

'Didn't you like her, Mum?'

'No, she's too pretty by far to be a school-teacher!'

Alex giggled. 'She's better than old Madame Montaner with her moustache and her garlic breath.'

Kelly gave him a sharp look. 'At least I knew where I was with Madame Montaner.'

'What does that mean?'

'Nothing.'

'Am I too young to know about it?'

'That's about it, Alex, yes.'

'That's what you always say.'

She leapt at him with a growl and he ran off squealing, with her giving chase. They had no idea that they were being observed until Tricot came bounding down to join in the fun. Kelly had captured Alex and was carrying him back to the house over her shoulder, both of them laughing uproariously.

As they reached the gate, she happened to look up and saw the shepherd on the hillside. He looked relaxed with his hands on his hips, one foot raised, resting on a grassy hummock. The day was warm and sunny so he was only wearing a T-shirt tucked into his jeans.

She saw his head nod in her direction and a hand came up in salute. He was too far away to see if he was smiling, but she thought that he probably was and smiled back. Then he whistled to Tricot and the dog obediently returned to him.

⋆   ⋆   ⋆

Half an hour later, Kelly was still trying to persuade the stove to stay lit.

'What is wrong with this thing? *Merde!*' She lashed out with her foot and gave the thing a kick, which didn't help, but it made her feel better.

'Maybe it's cursed,' Alex said from his seat on the back porch where he was keeping a vigil with his binoculars for anything that moved. 'Maybe that woman at the café put a fluence on it or something. She looked like a witch.'

'A what . . . ?' Kelly's mouth snapped shut at the sound of someone knocking loudly on the front door. She really didn't want any more visitors when she was in such a mess.

'*Bonjour!*' a voice called, and the dark brown tones of the shepherd's voice took her by surprise as she hurried from the back of the house to the front, frantically scrubbing at her sooty face with hands that were equally sooty.

'*Monsieur Borotra! Bonjour!*'

He was standing on the doorstep, looking very big, silhouetted as he was against the morning sun that was coming in from the east and glancing off his bare head, burnishing his rich, dark hair. He was clean-shaven today and looked quite handsome in a rugged sort of way.

He leaned against the doorpost, looking amused. For a moment, this threw her, then she remembered that she must look like a dirty chimney sweep.

'Do you need some help?' he asked, trying to hide his amusement.

'I'm sure it's just a case of getting used to things,' she said. 'I've been trying to light the stove in the kitchen, but for some reason it doesn't want to work.'

'Ah.' He pointed to his own cheek and his grin widened. 'That explains the black make-up! It is an old enemy, that stove, but we are well acquainted. Let me do it for you.'

'Oh, but — I mean, it's very kind, but . . . ' She really didn't want to be thought of as a helpless female. Even worse, she didn't want him thinking she was forcing herself on him five minutes after she moved in. 'I don't want to keep you back.'

'No problem! Today is my day off. Remi Dubois looks after my sheep on Sundays, except when he cannot get out of his bed because of rheumatism.'

'Well . . . ' Kelly hesitated, uncertain.

He shrugged and spread his hands wide. Like the rest of him, his hands were big.

'It is your choice, *madame*, but I lived in this house for many years. I know how things work.'

She gave a small, self-conscious laugh and stepped back so he could enter. In doing so she caught a glimpse of her reflection in the glass of the front door and groaned at her black face with its white rings around her eyes.

Alex had banged on the metal tube that ran from the stove up the chimney, saying that it was probably blocked. And he was probably right, too, because a whole lot of soot had come shooting down at her just as she stuck her head in to see if she could see the sky.

'Don't worry about it.' Jean-Paul Borotra was still grinning and trying to tone it down to a polite smile. 'It happens.'

She led the way to the kitchen, grabbed a brush and swept away the dirt from in front of the stove. He knelt down, and minutes later the whole thing flared into life with not a bit of smoke or soot to be seen.

Kelly sighed. 'You obviously have the right touch. What was I doing wrong?'

'Nothing so terrible. You had simply not operated the damper.'

'The damper?'

'Uh-huh.' He came and pointed to

the side of the stove. 'That little thing there. It is fully open now. When the fire is burning fiercely, you must close it to halfway. If you want the fire to burn slowly — through the night, for example — you can close it down completely. *Voilà!*'

'As simple as that, eh?'

'And . . . ' He indicated the fire itself and she waited to hear what else she had not done right. 'You must use dry sticks to light it.'

The fire was already taking the chill off the kitchen, which was cold despite the warmth of the sun outside.

'I'm so grateful,' she said. 'At least now I can boil water. Can I offer you a cup of coffee?'

He glanced at his watch and gave an apologetic smile. 'Thank you, but no. I have a *rendezvous*. Perhaps another time.'

'Yes, of course. Thank you, Monsieur Borotra, for . . . '

'Please — I am Jean-Paul.'

She was aware that she was running

her fingers through her tangle of hair. She always did that when she was embarrassed, and now her hair must be as black as her face. Good Lord, how gauche she must appear.

He gave a Gallic shrug and his dark brows went up. '*À bientôt, alors.*'

Kelly stood listening to him having a few words with Alex. She was so glad it was Jean-Paul and not Yvette Bernardi who was her neighbour. On the other hand, she would have been happier if Jean-Paul did not have to pass her door every time he came and went. His close proximity, for some reason that was beyond her, seemed to pose her a problem.

A Flash Of Jealousy

The furniture arrived a week late because of a string of mishaps and misunderstandings and the odd strike or two. However, Kelly was too relieved at having her own belongings around her at last to complain.

Alex, however, did have something to complain about.

'It's stupid not to have to go to school on Wednesdays,' he groused, his face unusually sulky.

'You must really like this school,' she said as she excavated her way into a packing crate containing her best china, 'to be complaining about a day off from it.'

'It's all right.'

'So it's not school you miss — and it can't be your new friends, because you could see them if you wanted to.'

'I know that.' Alex shrugged and

went on monotonously tapping his pen on the writing block in front of him.

'In that case, it must be that teacher of yours. Oh, Alex, you haven't got a crush on her already, have you?'

Alex pulled a face, then turned so she couldn't see his blush, but it was too late. 'She's nice!'

'I'm glad to hear it, but don't forget that she's your teacher. And at a glance, I'd say she's even older than me.'

'But you're different! I mean, you're . . .'

'Your mother.'

'No, I didn't mean that. I mean — well, she's hot.'

Kelly blinked at him, then stared, then bent down and peered into his averted face, which he tried to hide from her by putting his head down on his folded arms. 'Stop it, Mum!'

'What do you know about 'hot', young man?'

'Nothing! Guillaume and François at school think she's hot too, that's all. All the boys do.'

He gave her a sly smile and she

wafted her hand over his cowlick. Hot, indeed!

Alex got up and went to the door. 'I'm going down into the village, Mum. Guillaume's grandmother has rabbits.'

'Have you done your homework?'

'Yes. It was easy.'

'It won't be so easy when you go to the *lycée*, so make the most of it while you're here. And stop thinking about Mademoiselle Bernardi. In a few years' time she might look just like Madame Montaner.'

'You're just jealous, Mum,' he said as a parting shot and disappeared fast before she could find something to throw at him.

Jealous? Kelly sighed. Oh, yes! She was jealous of any woman her age who could look so slim and alluring. She twisted in front of her wardrobe mirror to see how she looked from the back these days. It was a long time since she had cared. Peter had never seemed to take note of her appearance.

Not too bad, she thought. Slightly

well rounded, perhaps, but at least she went in and out where she was supposed to. Being thin wouldn't suit her all that well. The school-teacher had an advantage there. She had probably been born skinny.

Kelly came out of the house and did what she always did without thinking. She looked up at Jean-Paul's cottage. Why she had the impulse to do this, she didn't know. After all, he wasn't there during the day. He was up on the high pastures with his sheep and didn't get back until dusk. Every evening she heard his feet trudging past her house and on up the hill, but he never stopped.

★   ★   ★

It was midday and there were customers in the café. All of them were men. Except, of course, for Madame Soubirous, who gave Kelly a grim-faced stare as she entered. The hum of conversation stopped, heads turned and curious eyes stared at her.

Glasses were suspended halfway between table and lips.

'*Bonjour!*' Kelly greeted them shyly.

There were a few grunted responses, then Madame Soubirous put down the cloth she was wiping up with and stuck out her chin.

'*Oui?*'

'A glass of white wine, please,' Kelly said, in the hope that it would be better than the red wine she had tasted on her arrival.

The woman poured her a glass of Colombelle and put it down in front of her without their eyes meeting once. Kelly took a sip and found, with relief, that it was surprisingly good.

'Thank you. Is Monsieur Soubirous available, *madame?*' she ventured.

'What do you want with my husband?' Delphine's eyes flickered suspiciously over her, then concentrated on polishing the stainless steel of the coffee machine.

'Well, I believe he is the mayor.' Kelly smiled sweetly around her, keeping her voice just high enough for the listening audience to hear. 'I need to register officially with him — and I would like some advice. There's obviously quite a lot of work needs doing on the house.'

'Such as?'

Kelly resented the woman's unfriendly attitude, but she was determined not to show that it bothered her.

'Well, the electricity system is ancient and needs replacing.' She had plugged in the kettle while toasting a slice of bread yesterday and everything had gone 'clack'. 'And the roof leaks . . . ' She counted off the things needing attention.

'You will need more than an *artisan, madame,*' Delphine said with a wry smile. 'You will need an exorcist. The house has an evil spirit.'

There was a roar of laughter from the old men, who looked at each other and shook their heads. One man with a shiny bald pate and teeth like gravestones leaned across his table to a companion. 'If you ask me, it's Delphine who put the spell on the

61

house in the first place!' he muttered.

There was another burst of laughter and Delphine glowered at them.

'Armand!' she shouted in a deafening voice. 'Armand, the Englishwoman is here to see you.'

Armand Soubirous appeared, stretching, yawning and scratching his great belly. When he saw Kelly, he beamed delightedly at her.

'Ah, Madame Taylor! Welcome! You have a drink? Ah, yes! Ah, but the red is better. I will give you a bottle to take home with you.'

'Oh, there's no need, really,' Kelly said quickly and went on before he could insist: 'Monsieur Soubirous, I've come to register — and to ask you the names of some local *artisans*.'

Monsieur Soubirous' eyes brightened. He scratched his head and opened the flap at the end of the counter. 'Come through, *madame*. Come into my office.'

'Armand!' His wife was glaring at him with dark, accusing eyes. 'You have not put out the rubbish again. And you

62

have a meeting in five minutes at Gourette.'

Armand gave her a simpering smile. 'Since it will take me half an hour to get to Gourette, I am already late. My brother can wait. This way, Madame Taylor.'

The 'office' was a bare room with one bulging, rusting filing cabinet and a table covered with a stained yellow plastic cloth. There was, however, a reasonably modern computer. Armand sat down before this and invited her to occupy the chair opposite.

Looking at her, smiling, nodding, he placed a pair of bifocals on the tip of his nose and started prodding the computer keyboard, his tongue popping out with every prod. It seemed to take forever for him to find what he was looking for, then he sighed with great satisfaction and said, 'Ah! *Le voilá*! All this modernisation — it is so long-winded. In the old days, all we needed was a pencil and a piece of paper.'

With each answer she gave to his

questions, he uttered another 'Ah!' and pounded on the computer keyboard with two thick index fingers. She signed the necessary papers and then he regarded her fully, hands clasped over his paunch.

'Now! How can I help you, *madame?*'

She repeated her list of various house repairs and added that she would also need a plumber when she came to fit out a new bathroom.

'Oh, and there are quite a few jobs for a carpenter, if you know a good one.'

'A carpenter, *hein?*' He leaned back in his chair and she heard it creak dangerously beneath his weight. 'The best carpenter in these parts is the Basque.'

'Monsieur Borotra, do you mean?' Kelly asked, surprised.

'He has not always been a shepherd. He was once the carpenter of this village — a talented young man, but all that ended a long time ago . . . ' He spread his hands and raised his eyes to the ceiling.

'Oh, why was that?'

There was a slight pause and she could see Armand's brain working furiously, as if he realised he had spoken out of turn and was now regretting it.

'You are a stranger in our village, *madame*. You would not understand.'

'Perhaps not, Monsieur Soubirous,' Kelly said, getting to her feet because the stuffiness of the room and the lingering smell of onions were getting to her. 'But if he's a good carpenter . . . and it was his house, after all.'

'No, no! Better not, *hein!*' He put his finger up to his lips and glanced towards the door. 'I will give you the name of another.'

He scribbled names, addresses and numbers on a sheet of paper and handed it to her. She thanked him and started to leave, but when his hand was on the doorknob, he stopped, blocking her way with his bulk.

'I hear you have met my wife's niece, Yvette? She is the school-teacher here.'

'Yes, I have. My son is going to the school — just until the end of term. Then I must find a place for him at a *lycée*.'

'Yvette tells us that he is a very bright and willing child. She is very impressed with her English pupil.'

'I'm glad to know that.'

'She is pretty, *non?* For many years we have hoped that she will find happiness. There are men who would marry her tomorrow. Unfortunately, they do not please her. There is only one man for her and that, too, is unfortunate, but things can change.'

'I'm not sure that I follow you, Monsieur Soubirous. Is the man married?'

Monsieur Soubirous sucked in his mouth and shook his head.

'Not at all, but he is not the man Yvette's parents would want her to marry. You see, not only is he a foreigner, he was responsible for the death of Yvette's sister.' Then he smacked his forehead with the flat of his hand. 'I should not have divulged that. It was — indiscreet.'

Kelly was intrigued. 'Monsieur Soubirous — I know it's none of my business, but . . . '

The thick finger was pressed once more against his lips. 'I speak, of course, of Jean-Paul Borotra. The situation is difficult. All the same, my wife — the charming Delphine — is always afraid that Yvette will lose the man she loves to another. It would destroy her. You understand, I think, *madame?*'

'Yes, of course.'

Kelly felt slightly bemused. What was there for her to understand? If Yvette lost her Basque shepherd to someone else, it would hardly be *her* fault. Unless . . . ? Oh dear. They must see *her* as a threat! What a ridiculous thought.

'Jean-Paul Borotra,' Monsieur Soubirous said almost to himself and shook his head sadly. 'He was the one responsible for the death of little

Marie-Catherine. And now her sister is also in love with him. *Bizarre, non?*'

Bizarre, yes! Jean-Paul seemed such a quiet, gentle man. But then, what did they say about still waters running deep?

'Monsieur Soubirous, how did your niece die exactly?' she probed.

The mayor of Labadette looked away from her. He seemed to be upset and embarrassed at the same time.

'She died, Madame Taylor — and it was all Borotra's fault. I will say no more.'

'Armand!'

The cry came through from the bar and Armand Soubirous flinched. Then he put a guarded hand in front of his mouth as he leaned towards Kelly and whispered, 'But who am I to know about these things? And now, we must ask ourselves if the same fate awaits Yvette.'

He tapped the side of his long nose and nodded his head slowly. Then he was leading her out of his 'office', his hot hand supporting her elbow. The old men who were still in the bar followed their progress to the door, eyes laughing, mouths gaping and glasses in various stages of suspended animation.

Kelly walked away from the café with Armand Soubirous' words about Jean-Paul ringing in her head. She felt as if she were caught, suddenly, between the friendly, likeable shepherd on one side and, on the other, a family who accused him of causing a girl's death. The last thing she wanted was to get caught in the crossfire.

★ ★ ★

She didn't return immediately to the house, but spent time looking around the village. It was so peaceful. Although the doors and the windows of the houses were all thrown wide open to let in the sun, there was no sign of a living being, except one old, lazy dog.

The tolling of the church bell drew her steps in the direction of the tiny, squat building standing on its lonely promontory halfway up a grassy bank behind Labadette. Judging by the ancient design of the church it had to be at least eleventh century. The roof, with its small slate tiles, looked ready to crumble, and the stone walls beneath were worn and sculpted by the elements rather than a stonemason's hand.

The bell continued to toll out a steady, morbid 'dong — dong — dong'. The church itself was empty and dark, the gloomy chill of it sending a shiver through Kelly's bones. She found a steep, narrow flight of steps leading up to the graveyard, which was typically full of well-tended tombs covered in flowers.

A mutter of voices and the sound of digging reached her and as she rounded a corner she came to an abrupt halt. Two men were excavating a grave, watched by a tall priest in a flowing black soutane.

The priest had his back to her, but

sensed her presence. He swung around and came towards her, a tall skeleton of a man with morbid dark features. Kelly had to repress a shiver at the sight of him.

'I'm sorry, *mon pere*,' she apologised. 'I didn't mean to disturb you.'

He glared down at her from his great height, standing so close she was obliged to step back.

'You must be the Englishwoman they told me about,' he said, his voice low and sibilant. 'The one living in the Borotra house, *non?*'

'Yes, I'm Kelly Taylor.'

His long, spidery hand shot out and found hers. It was cold to the touch.

'I am the *curé* here — *l'Abbé* Pascal Lauga, but they call me simply *Pére Pascal*. Are you of the faith, my child?'

'No,' she said quickly, pulling her hand free. 'No, I'm Protestant.'

'Anglican, *hein?*' His eyes burned into her and she shuddered.

'Has there been a death in the village?' she asked, peering around him at the two diggers.

The priest inclined his head. 'Old Monsieur Dieuzeide. Two months ago.'

Kelly started to nod, then did a double-take as she realised what he had said. 'Two months ago?'

It was common knowledge that the French lost no time in burying their dead. There was even a joke that people liked to tell, saying that if you felt tired in France it was better not to lie down in a public place or you might wake up talking to the worms.

Again, the skull head of the priest inclined. 'Yes, it is very unfortunate. Monsieur Dieuzeide's family have only just discovered that their grandfather was not buried in the right place. He left strict instructions that he should be placed with his head towards the Pic du Midi d'Ossau and his feet towards the village. It is never a good idea to go against the dying wishes of a loved one, *hein?*'

'I suppose not,' Kelly said, then gave him a bright smile. 'Well, it was nice meeting you, Père Pascal, I must get back.'

'Yes, of course. Your husband is with you at Labadette?'

'My husband and I are separated.'

'Ah! One day I will visit you.'

Over my dead body, Kelly was thinking as she hurried away, suppressing a shudder.

★　★　★

'So! How was your day, young man?' Kelly greeted her son when he returned later that afternoon.

'Great! Can we get some rabbits?'

'Rabbits? What for?'

Alex stuck his hands in his pockets and did a soft-shoe shuffle that reminded Kelly to clean the grit from the floor. It seemed to enter into the house no matter what she did.

'Guillaume's grandmother has lots. You start with just two, then you get *loads* of them.'

She eyed him cautiously. 'Alex, have

you thought about why Guillaume's grandmother has *loads* of rabbits? I mean, what she has them for?'

'No.'

'They — um — er . . . Well, they — um — eat them.'

She could tell by the creased expression on Alex's face that he was upset.

'They can't do that!' he cried.

'I'm sorry, but why else do you think they keep them? It's not because they're cute — and I admit they are very cute — but it's like sheep and cows. They breed them for food.'

'Maybe just one?' There was a pleading note that she felt was hard to resist.

'We'll see,' she told him and received a grateful hug. 'So, don't you want to know what your mum did while you were playing with those cuddly, self-reproductive machines?'

Kelly had the urge to talk to somebody, but she didn't have a telephone installed yet so she couldn't call the one person she would enjoy a one-to-one girly with, her sister, Sylvie, to whom she told all.

'So, what did you do this afternoon, Mum?' Alex obliged with a mischievous grin.

'Well,' she said, getting out bread and jam for his afternoon snack, 'I visited the mayor and made sure that they know we exist officially in Labadette.'

'Mademoiselle Bernardi says it takes a long time for strangers to be accepted,' he informed her. 'The Basque has been here for thirty years and they still think of him as a foreigner.'

'She told you that — about Monsieur Borotra?'

Alex was shaking his head. 'It wasn't Mademoiselle Bernardi who said that. It was Guillaume. He said that Jean-Paul came to live with his grandparents when he was a little boy. They lived here in this house. He was an orphan. His grandparents were Basque too, but they had lived here a long time. When he was twenty-five he got engaged to Mademoiselle Bernardi's sister, but she died. Now everybody says he'll marry Mademoiselle Bernardi because it's not good for a man to be on his own for so long.'

'Well, I see you're getting to know quite a bit about this village from your friend Guillaume.'

He shrugged. 'He's cool. What else did you do?'

'Oh, I went up to look at the little graveyard on the hill and met a spooky priest. They were burying some old man for the second time, and judging by the appearance of the priest it might have been some black magic ritual for all I know. I could imagine him flying around here in the middle of the night, flapping bat wings!'

Settling In

The following Sunday, Kelly was awake early, having slept badly. She wandered out onto the terrace in her housecoat in time to see an old man plodding up the track. As he approached, he touched a gnarled finger to his black beret and nodded, giving her a cheerful, but largely toothless smile. He went on up to Jean-Paul's cottage then returned a few minutes later and gave her a curious look.

'*Bonjour, monsieur!*'

'*Bonjour, madame! Ça va?*'

'*Oui, ça va, merci.*'

The old Frenchman whipped off his beret and made a small bow in her direction. 'I am Remi Doubois, madame. I am retired for a long time now, but I help Jean-Paul with his sheep.' His head nodded in the direction of the cottage. 'I used to own many animals — two hundred, three! Goats too! It is a tradition that is dying, like many in the Pyrénées. We can no longer make our goats' cheeses and sell them to the public. We must bow down before European Commission rules. The next to go will be the *brebis* — the best cheese in France. We used to be eighteen shepherds in this valley. Now, we are two. It is sad, no?'

'Yes,' Kelly told him. 'It's very sad.'

'Ach! Progress!' He threw his hands up in the air and ambled back down the track towards the main road that would take him up another thousand feet into the mountains where Jean-Paul's sheep were grazing.

'Mum?' Alex was hanging over the rail of the balcony above her head. 'Can we have a goat? We can make our own cheese and . . . '

'Keep trying, Alex! One of these days you might hit lucky and find an animal we can keep without too much bother.'

'Sheep then?' Alex persisted. 'Guillaume says that sheep give the best cheese milk of all. Maybe Jean-Paul will let us have one of his.'

'No, Alex.'

'Well, if you marry the Basque, Mum . . . ' he began, but he got no further before Kelly cut him off.

'Alex Taylor, I have no intention of marrying anyone!' she shouted up at him. 'Besides, I'm still married to your father . . . '

'But you're getting a divorce!'

'Yes, but . . . '

'So, you *could* marry Jean-Paul. Yes?'

She hadn't seen a movement. Not even out of the corner of her eye. She hadn't heard a footfall. But suddenly there he was, standing beside her, and Alex was grinning cheekily down on the pair of them.

'Goodness — Monsieur Borotra!' She felt her face going scarlet.

The Basque smiled, his eyes lighting up with amusement. 'I did not mean to startle you.'

'Startle me? Oh, no, but — um — I'm sorry about all that . . . ' She waved a hand in Alex's direction and the boy ducked back into his room. 'That was just Alex being stupid. He likes to embarrass me.'

'He is a boy. It is normal.'

She turned to look at him, perhaps scrutinising his face thoroughly for the first time. 'I can't imagine that you were ever like that, Jean-Paul.'

He laughed. He had a nice laugh, deep and throaty.

'Here — I have something for you, to welcome you into our midst.'

Kelly blinked at him as he held up some delicately carved bone chimes strung from a solid wooden disc of pine that was honed and polished to a golden shine. As he moved it before her eyes it jingled in the most delicate of tones.

'Why, it's beautiful! I love chimes, but . . . ' She frowned at him. 'You really don't have to give me gifts.'

'It's an old tradition. They say the chimes keep away the evil spirits. My grandmother always had some — to protect her — there!' He indicated a point above Kelly's head, and when she looked she could see the remnants of a fine cord that had once supported something, but was now fluttering aimlessly in the morning breeze. 'If you have some steps I will fix these in place for you.'

'All right — thank you — oh!' Kelly had suddenly realised that she was still in her housecoat. 'Excuse me!'

She heard him chuckle as she dived back inside the house and flew up the stairs to jump into a tracksuit before finding him a pair of stepladders. She also took the time to brush her hair and scrub a damp sponge around her face, which was already showing signs of a tan since she had been working in the garden for a few days.

'Here you are.' She arrived back on the terrace a trifle breathlessly with a short pair of ladders. 'Sorry about that. I'm not used to visitors so early in the morning.'

'No problem,' he assured her.

The stepladders creaked when he put

his weight on them, but he didn't seem to notice, and the chimes were soon tinkling gently above their heads.

'It's such a pretty sound,' she said.

'Now you are safe from gremlins and vampires and witches' curses,' he said with just a touch of humour creasing the sun-bronzed skin around his eyes.

'Jean-Paul, did your grandmother think her house was haunted?'

'No! She was too wise for that.' He glanced towards the village, then his eyes were upon her and they stared intently. 'What have they been telling you, the good people of Labadette?'

She felt herself colour beneath his scrutiny.

'Nothing very much. Actually, it was just something Madame Soubirous said — about this house.'

'Ah! Delphine believes she is an authority on most things. My grandmother did not have time for the woman. What she says — it is not necessarily true.'

'Are you saying she is a liar?'

'No, not a liar. She tells the truth as she sees it, but she does not always see it the way it is. However, she is powerful in the village. Where Delphine Soubirous leads, the other women will follow.'

'Including her niece, the school-teacher?' She couldn't help herself. The question just jumped out of her mouth and she saw a shadow flit across his face.

'Yvette? No, she is too strong-willed, but that also poses a problem.' He glanced up and over Kelly's shoulder as Alex came bounding down the stairs eager to enjoy the day. 'Ah, it is good to see a boy so lively at this early hour.'

'*Bonjour, monsieur!*' Alex sang out as he joined them on the porch. 'Are you going up to the *plateau* to be with your sheep?'

Jean-Paul nodded. 'It just so happens that I am. Normally I do not work on Sundays, but there is a problem with the spring that supplies fresh water to the sheep. It is blocked, so I must go up there today and free it.

Alex's eyes widened with interest. 'Can I come with you?'

'Alex!' Kelly said, amazed that her son should be so forward.

The shepherd smiled and ruffled a hand over Alex's mop of unruly hair. 'He is welcome to accompany me, with your permission? But he will be expected to work.'

'Oh, Mum, can I?'

'Well, I . . . ' Kelly looked at Jean-Paul and found his eyes shining. He wasn't just being polite. He looked as if he actually liked the idea of Alex going with him. 'If you're sure?'

'I am sure,' Jean-Paul said.

'Mum?'

'All right, all right!' Kelly relented. 'But you be careful, Alex, and don't get in Jean-Paul's way.'

Alex nodded solemnly, then rushed off to pack some bread and cheese and fruit into a backpack, as well as a book to read and a pocket computer game.

'I'm ready, Jean-Paul,' Alex said, reappearing a few minutes later. He grimaced when Kelly insisted he take his lightweight waterproof. However, when Jean-Paul said it was a good idea, he stuffed it in his backpack without further argument.

Kelly watched the pair of them march off together, smiling at the jaunty way Alex kept up with the big Frenchman, all the while grinning happily at her over his shoulder and waving until they disappeared at the end of the track.

She spent the morning working in the garden, but, the afternoon being hot and idyllic, she took her sketchpad and drew the village as seen from on high. She sketched, she rested, drank some water, read a few pages of a paperback and generally enjoyed being lazy, though it was strange not having Alex around.

She packed up her things at five o'clock and wondered how her son was faring. Alex was like a friendly puppy, liking everyone. But maybe she should have discouraged him from going up to the high pastures with Jean-Paul. After all, they hardly knew the man and . . .

Her stomach churned slightly as she recalled Delphine Soubirous' words regarding her niece. The one who was not the school-teacher. Jean-Paul had caused the girl's death, she had said. But how? He seemed perfectly amiable and gentle, despite his size. If he had harmed the girl in any way, surely he wouldn't be walking around free now?

Anyway, she was sure Alex would be all right. What could possibly happen to him up there on the side of the mountain with Jean-Paul and the old man, Tricot and two hundred sheep? Delphine was probably the type of woman who could see evil in everything and her opinion of Jean-Paul was coloured by her dislike of his Basque grandparents.

As she was nearing the house, Kelly saw a tall, slim figure descend the hill from the cottage. Yvette Bernardi was wearing a long flowing skirt of a white silky material dotted with yellow sun-flowers. It was split in places, showing off her long slender legs as she walked.

'*Bon soir*, Yvette!' Kelly called out as she came nearer. 'If you are looking for Jean-Paul, he is up on the high pastures today. There's a problem with a spring to sort out.'

'You seem to know a lot about Jean-Paul's business,' Yvette said coldly, her eyes narrowing.

'Only because he's taken Alex with him,' Kelly told her, feeling the heat go out of the day as the other woman's eyes cut into her like ice.

Yvette continued staring at her for a moment or two, then turned briskly and marched away.

* * *

It was well past seven when Kelly caught sight of Jean-Paul, Remi and Tricot coming down off the hill. She had been getting anxious, and after her initial relief at seeing the pair of black berets bobbing along the track in the distance, she started to panic when she couldn't see Alex. Then she realised that Jean-Paul was carrying the boy on his back. The boy must be too exhausted to walk, she decided. Jean-Paul had said he would have to work hard, and it looked like he hadn't been joking.

Smiling, she went halfway down the track to meet them. The old man grinned widely and she noticed he was carrying Alex's backpack as well as his own and Jean-Paul's.

Jean-Paul gave her a reassuring smile, but she noticed he didn't offer to set Alex on his feet. For his part, Alex looked very tired and drained of colour. He gave her a sheepish smile and that was when she noticed that his ankle was bandaged heavily.

'I bring you one very tired apprentice shepherd who has worked hard all day,' Jean-Paul told her. 'Don't worry — the ankle is not broken, just slightly twisted. He tripped.'

'I didn't see the hole in the ground,' Alex muttered. 'Jean-Paul carried me all the way down the mountain, Mum. He's as strong as an ox.'

'Even so, I'm sure the last thing he wanted to do at the end of a tiring day was to walk for miles with you on his back, Alex,' she scolded mildly. 'You should be more careful, I'm always telling you. He's so clumsy . . . ' she added to the two men.

Jean-Paul strode into the house and put Alex down gently on the old settee, which Kelly had kept, though she couldn't imagine why. He straightened his back with a slight grunt, then turned to face her.

'It's not serious. Put some ice on it if you have any.'

'I'm sorry that you've had the bother of . . . '

'It was not a bother, really! He's a good boy — so willing! He was a good help to me and to Remi up on the mountain.'

Then he turned back to Alex and the

89

smile he gave the boy was warm and genuine. 'When the *vacances* come I will teach you how to be a real shepherd, if you are still interested.'

'Aw, yes! Yes, please! That'll be great!'

Kelly wasn't so sure about that. She had never envisaged her rather fragile-looking son getting a liking for a tough outdoors life, even during the holidays. Nature watching was one thing, but working alongside Jean-Paul in the high pastures of a rugged mountain was something else again.

As she walked back to the door with Jean-Paul, he touched her arm and spoke softly. 'Don't worry. He will be all right. He is lacking some masculine influence in his life. Working out on the mountain for a few weeks — it will make a man of him.'

'That's all very well, but he's only ten years old. Isn't it like throwing him in at the deep end? Besides, I'm not sure I want my son to end up as a shepherd . . . '

She could have bitten her tongue off

as soon she spoke. It must have seemed like an insult to him, yet he continued to smile even after he flinched slightly at her remark.

'The boy needs experience of life other than at his mother's side. Of course, if you object, I will respect your wishes. Now, Remi and I are going to the café for a drink and a bowl of *garbure*, which, unlike the wine, I can thoroughly recommend.' The thick vegetable soup was apparently one of the café's specialities.

'Perhaps I'll try it one day,' Kelly said, then remembered Yvette's visit. 'By the way, your fiancée was here. She seemed surprised not to find you.'

'My . . . ?' He looked puzzled.

'Yvette Bernardi.'

'She came to the cottage?' Jean-Paul's eyebrows shot up and Remi chewed on his sagging mouth and tried to look disinterested. 'I'll speak to her later.'

'Jean-Paul!' Alex called out. 'Next time we go up the mountain, can Mum come too? You'll love it, Mum! We saw lots of marmots and izards. It was great!'

Jean-Paul shrugged. 'One day perhaps. Why not?'

Kelly tried not to show too much excitement at the prospect.

★ ★ ★

It was wonderful being connected to the outside world again. Kelly sat looking at her newly-installed telephone, fingers hovering eagerly over the buttons. She had told Peter she would contact him as soon as they were settled. Even though she thought he was a bit of a heel, she had no intention of there being a war between them that might affect Alex.

She wasn't yet in the mood, however, to speak to her estranged husband, though she would have to do it sometime. He was the father of her only child and he had agreed to share the overall responsibility — albeit from a distance.

Kelly glanced at the clock over the

mantelpiece. It was a bad time to phone her sister, who would just be getting home from work. She would be stressed because she didn't get on with her boss, and Robert, the house-husband of the year, would also be stressed, because being domestic wasn't really his cup of tea. However, he didn't have a choice because he was out of work and Sylvie wasn't.

It was no good. Kelly just had to speak to someone sympathetic or burst. And Sylvie was the perfect choice, so never mind the hour.

'Sylvie! Hi! It's me!'

'Kelly! Are you all right?' The voice at the other end was ten octaves higher than normal as it screamed out down the hundreds of miles that separated the two sisters.

'I'm fine, Sylvie. How are you?'

'Three of the four Munchkins have measles. Robert's broken his arm showing Munchkin number four how to skateboard, and I'm starting a rotten cold.'

'Sounds pretty normal to me. How's the job?'

'Stinking! I hate it, I hate the boss and I'd give it all up tomorrow if we didn't need the money. But enough about us. What's been happening to the French branch of the family?'

Kelly took a deep breath. 'I love the house and the scenery's great!' she said enthusiastically.

'That's good. What about the locals? Made any new friends yet?'

'They're a bit on the eccentric side. Alex likes his new school, though, and he's made friends with the local shepherd who lives near us.'

'Don't tell me — old fella with cracking joints and missing teeth, smelling of sheep dip and worse?'

Kelly allowed herself a big grin, not that her sister could see it.

'No, actually he's about thirty-eight, dark, wears his hair in a pony-tail and has a body to write home about.'

'Shoulders?'

'Mm. And thighs.'

'Better and better! Peter always looked like a piece of wet string with knots. So, this shepherd — a pony-tail! I thought you didn't like that sort of thing.'

'I don't, but I have to admit, on him it looks great.'

'Tell me more!'

'He's a Basque by the name of Jean-Paul Borotra who has some kind of mysterious past here in the village. But he's very nice, really. He's quiet, a bit on the shy side — and he's engaged to the village school-teacher.'

'I hate her!'

'Actually, she doesn't put out very likeable vibes. I can see what *she* sees in *him*, but for the life of me, I can't see what *he* sees in *her*!'

Sylvie laughed wickedly. 'Kelly, you like him, don't you?'

'Don't be ridiculous. He's only a shepherd!' Why was she blushing? 'Anyway, I'm not looking for a new relationship. It's too soon.'

'Nonsense! It would be the best thing

to help you get over Peter.'

'I got over Peter a long time ago.'

'Well, you know what I mean. You need a bit of romance to liven up your existence — make you feel part of the living world again.'

'Do you think so, Sylvie? I'm not sure about that.'

'Isn't there anybody else?'

'What? In this village? There's Remi, who looks about eighty, and there's Armand, the mayor, who's fat and greasy and married to Delphine who doesn't like anybody, especially foreigners. I swear, Sylvie, there isn't anybody single and under the age of seventy who's anywhere near interesting. Anyway, I'd rather do without.'

'I'd like to hear you say that again in six months' time,' Sylvie said.

'Honestly, I just couldn't stand the emotional upheaval,' Kelly told her. 'Right now, I feel free, and it's wonderful after all those years with Peter. He hasn't rung by any chance, has he?'

There was a short silence, then her

sister took a deep breath. 'Well, yes, as a matter of fact he has. He rings all the time. He's desperate to know what's happening to you and Alex. I think he really cares.'

'That's new. He never seemed to care when we were under his nose.'

'Under his thumb, you mean.' Sylvie had never liked her brother-in-law.

'Is he still at the flat?' Kelly enquired.

'As far as I know, yes.'

'I suppose I should give him a ring. The summer holidays are coming up. He might want Alex to go and spend some time with him in London.'

Kelly had been thinking about that a lot lately. She wasn't sure it was a good thing, but she couldn't stand in Peter's way. He was Alex's father and had his rights. Just because he had thrown her over for an older woman it didn't mean Alex couldn't go and spend time with him.

'Kelly?' Sylvie sounded anxious. 'What if Peter doesn't want Alex for the holidays?'

Kelly sighed. 'Actually I don't think it'll be a problem. Alex has his mind set on becoming a shepherd and Jean-Paul is more than ready to teach him.'

'He sounds like a nice kind of guy.'

'Yes, he is . . . '

'Hmm.'

'Don't start, Sylvie. I told you, he's already spoken for.'

They went on to talk of more mundane things and ended up laughing like schoolgirls. The moment she hung up, Kelly felt again a sense of emptiness.

The Truth About His Past

The short spring burgeoned into full summer and the temperatures rose, though with the mountains so close, there was always a breath of cool air, morning and evening. The days, however, were long and languid and sometimes Kelly felt sapped of energy as she lounged on the veranda, a glass of something cool in her hand, a book open on her lap, her eyes shaded as she gazed towards the distant peaks, now almost totally devoid of snow.

She sketched regularly and contacted the agencies with whom she had worked before her marriage to Peter. Most of them had never heard of her, having changed editors several times over in the last ten years. A small handful asked her to send samples of her work in, and out of those, only two finally showed any real interest.

She wasn't exactly short of money, but she felt the need to work. She needed something to occupy her hands as well as her mind.

It was July and Alex was spending more and more time with Jean-Paul and Remi. Occasionally he saw his school chums in the village, but being up in the pastures with the sheep was what he really liked. Jean-Paul had become his hero. He could barely open his mouth without the shepherd's name dripping from his lips.

'Did you know, Mum, that when the sheep have lambs, Jean-Paul has to milk them every few hours? That's how he gets the milk to make the *brebis* cheese, and he does that himself, too. His cheese is famous and there's even a shepherd over in Spain who says that Jean-Paul's cheese is superior.'

'I'm glad to hear it,' Kelly said with a laugh. They had tasted some of Jean-Paul's cheese and it certainly was delicious.

'And he knows the names of all the

wild flowers and plants on the mountain. He sketches them in a little notebook, then he carves them into wood. I've seen him do it, with a little tool thing. He does it in between moving the sheep around. He has to keep moving them to make sure they get the best grass to graze on — and they wander a bit, so Tricot and me have to round them up — like cowboys, but I suppose we're actually sheep-boys . . .

'Yes. When the sheep go up to the really high pastures, Jean-Paul stays with them all the time. He's got a stone cottage. When he goes up the mountain, Mum, can I go with him and stay overnight at the cottage?'

'That sounds wonderful, Alex, but I think even Jean-Paul would draw the line at that. Besides, I could do with your help down here for a change. And you're going to have to prepare for going to the *lycée* soon.'

Kelly was the first to admit that Alex was looking better and seemed much healthier and stronger since he spent his days working on the mountain. At first, she would only agree to him going when the weather was good. However, he soon became so obsessed that it was virtually impossible to keep him in the house, come rain or shine. He started accompanying Jean-Paul in all weathers and far from falling ill, as she had expected, he seemed to thrive on it.

Persuading him that he really did need to spend a week or two with his father in London hadn't been easy, but Alex agreed in the end. Peter had been slightly ambivalent about it, even though it had been his suggestion.

'Mum, the sheep are going to be moved again next week,' Alex called from the bathroom, where he was soaking in the bath, turning into a pale, stewed prune. Though he wasn't so pale these days. He had a tan to be proud of and his fair hair was bleached to straw blonde on top, making his blue eyes more vivid than ever.

'Really?' Kelly came to the open

doorway and leaned against the support.

'Yes, they're going even farther up the mountain to the really high pastures. At the moment they're on the plateau — or the *pont*. That's the middle bit. In the big heat they go right up as far as they can get and that's when Jean-Paul has to stay with them most of the time. He says there are foxes, and last year he even saw a wolf!'

'A wolf! I thought they were just in the Alps.'

'Jean-Paul says they've introduced them into our end of the Pyrénées and they're starting to breed. Isn't that super?'

'I doubt if Jean-Paul thinks it's super.'

'He says he has great respect for wolves and that they're not as dangerous as they've been made out to be in the past.'

Kelly smiled at her son who had grown at least three inches that summer and filled out so that he no longer looked so frail. She had Jean-Paul to thank for that. One day he would be a wonderful father to his children, if he had any.

Kelly often wondered about his relationship with the teacher. She saw him often enough, but he never talked about his private life. He did small repair jobs for her in his spare time. She never asked him to do the work. He just seemed to sense that it needed doing and did it. He was good with his hands and was happy working with wood. Once she had taken a peek inside his cottage and been amazed at how clean and tidy it was and how the place reflected his love of woodcarving. The furniture was all hand-made and, Alex assured her, was all Jean-Paul's work.

Alex was squeezing the softened bar of soap in his fingers, singing softly to himself as he watched it shoot into the air and come back down with a splash.

'I think it's time you got out before you start to shrink,' she told him, holding out a thick bath towel.

Alex looked at her and pulled a face. 'Jean-Paul wants you to go up the mountain with us tomorrow, since it's going to be my last day.'

Kelly had wondered if the Basque would remember the invitation he had issued all those weeks ago. She had pushed it to the back of her mind, telling herself that it was just one of those polite invitations that people feel obliged to issue, then never follow up.

'Did Jean-Paul say that, or are you just making it up to make me feel better?' she asked.

Alex gave her a lop-sided smile that was very much one of Jean-Paul's expressions. She saw the Frenchman's influence on her son more and more these days.

'He said he would like you to come with us, but he's afraid to ask you because you're such a lady and . . . '

' 'Such a lady', indeed! What does he mean by that?'

'I don't know, but he's always asking about you.'

'Does he ever talk about Mademoiselle Bernardi?'

Alex stepped out of the bath, wrapping the towel tightly around his lithe body. He shook his head. 'I don't think he sees her any more. They had a fight.'

'He told you that?'

'No, but one day he was really angry. He wouldn't tell me why, but I heard him muttering about 'that Yvette'. Are you going to come with us tomorrow? He said to tell you to bring a picnic if you are.'

'You're going to miss him, aren't you, Alex?'

Alex went strangely quiet and sulky as he rubbed himself dry and struggled into his boxer shorts. It was too warm at night now to wear anything else.

'I would like to go with him, but he won't let me, just like you said. He said you wouldn't like it, and besides, he thought I should stay and look after you.'

'Well, that was thoughtful anyway.'

Kelly laughed. 'Not that I need you to look after me, young man, but it's time you came down from your mountain and made friends again in the village. It's not good for you to spend so much time with grown-ups. You need to be with children of your own age.'

'Guillaume's all right. The others are too, but . . . ' His voice tailed off.

'But you would rather be with Jean-Paul? Why is that? What do the pair of you talk about when you're up there on the mountain?'

'All sorts of things. He knows a lot of history — the Basques, Eleanor of Aquitaine, the French Revolution. And he likes music and art. Toulouse Lautrec once painted his great-grandfather.'

'He likes music?'

'Uh-huh, but it's the classical stuff — you know, the kind you listen to after I've gone to bed.'

Kelly often sat alone into the small hours of the morning listening to her collection of CDs — Mozart, Bizet, Sibelius. Peter hadn't shared her tastes

107

at all. He preferred modern jazz — discordant, like their marriage had been.

'This hero of yours, Jean-Paul — he's got a lot of hidden qualities. What else does he do?'

'He reads a lot. There's a wall-full of books in his cottage. He doesn't have a telly though, or a computer. It's all pretty prehistoric up there.'

'Hallelujah!' Kelly clapped her hands and laughed, remembering how Peter used to spend his evenings, when he was at home, with his eyes glued to the computer screen and his fingers flying over the keys as he feverishly surfed the Internet and called up his Stock Exchange figures and 'chatted' to scientific groups. He had been completely addicted.

'So? Are you going tomorrow?'

Kelly regarded him seriously. '*You* don't seem very enthusiastic about the idea, Alex,' she said and he coloured slightly. 'But at the risk of disappointing you — just try keeping me away!'

'Oh! Right — super!' He was forcing his eagerness and she guessed that he had hoped to have Jean-Paul to himself on his last day on the mountain, but she wasn't going to give up the opportunity of a few hours in such interesting company.

★   ★   ★

'He's coming!' Alex came bounding into the kitchen. He watched her packing the last of the items for the day into her backpack and hopped impatiently from foot to foot. 'Come on!'

'All right, Alex, I'm coming,' she told him with a small, smiling frown. 'Don't get so agitated.'

'If you're not ready, he might go without you.'

'I hardly think it'll hurt him to hang on for a couple of seconds, Alex.'

There was a tinkling bell sound from the veranda as Jean-Paul's head brushed against the chimes, then a short rat-a-tat on the doorpost.

'*J'arrive!*' Kelly called out and heaved the backpack on to her shoulders, wishing it weighed less.

'*Salut, Jean-Paul!*' she heard Alex greet the shepherd.

Jean-Paul was already standing on the track by the time she arrived. He turned to regard her, his small canvas backpack taking up no room at all on his broad back.

'I hope you have trousers with you,' he said with a nod at her knees, naked below her shorts. 'It is already hot and you risk being burned.'

'I think I've thought of everything,' she said, indicating her pack.

They had gone a few hundred yards up the mountain when Jean-Paul, who had been fairly quiet until then, stopped and waited for her to catch him up. Alex was striding out ahead and didn't even notice that his hero was no longer keeping pace with him.

'Let me have your backpack,' Jean-Paul said, holding out a hand to haul Kelly up a particularly steep gradient

110

where the grass was damp and spongy and the stones slippery.

Just as he gripped her hand, her feet went from under her and he lifted her clear, swinging her up, so that she left the ground and landed beside him, thudding against his hard chest.

'I'm all right, really!' she objected, but he was already relieving her of her backpack and slinging it on to his own shoulders, before striding off again.

Kelly followed behind, relieved to get rid of the weight, but irritated at showing him what a weakling she was. Rather than spend the rest of the climb dwelling on this humiliation, however, she tried to concentrate on other, unrelated things.

'OK! We take a break here!' Jean-Paul indicated a grassy mound.

Thank goodness! Kelly sank down, feeling her feet throb and the blood pound up to her head. Alex, hearing the command, turned and looked at them in disbelief. 'We don't usually stop before we get to the sheep,' he objected sulkily.

'We stop today.'

'Why?'

'Because I say.' Jean-Paul beckoned to the lad and sat down beside Kelly, leaving only inches between them. She could feel the heat emanating from his body, smell the soapy, laundered freshness of his blue shirt. 'Come, Alex. It is hot today. It is necessary to take it in easy stages.'

'Please don't feel you have to stop for me,' she said and he gave her a quick glance.

'It is not a problem,' he said, then: 'So! What do you have in this bag of yours?'

'A flask of coffee,' she told him hopefully and he took the hint.

'Fine! Coffee right now would be good.'

They sat drinking black coffee in a silence that wasn't exactly companionable. At least, she didn't know how Jean-Paul felt about it, but she felt decidedly uncomfortable. Part of her wanted to talk, get closer, get to know him better. The other part of her was holding itself at bay, telling her that to get closer to any man, but especially to Jean-Paul, was dangerous and would only end in trouble.

'That was good!' He handed her his empty cup. 'I thought the English made only instant coffee and then drowned it in milk!'

'Some do, but not all of us.'

'I can see I have a lot to learn — about the English. The boy tells me that he is going back to England tomorrow.'

'That's right. He's a bit reluctant, which is probably why he's in a bad mood today. You've had a great impact on my son, Jean-Paul.'

The shepherd shrugged and looked away. 'He is a good boy, but I am sorry if I have caused trouble between him and his father.'

Kelly shook her head, feeling that he was watching her out of the corner of his eye. 'It's not your fault. Alex and Peter never got on. Actually, I'm grateful to you for taking him in hand. He looks so much better these days.'

'Can we go now?' came the shout from Alex, who was already moving on up the mountain without waiting for them.

Jean-Paul got to his feet and pulled Kelly up after him. His hand was big and hard and strong and the heat from it made her quiver slightly.

She glanced surreptitiously at him as he bent to do up the backpack and heave it on to his shoulder. He was tough, and not nearly as refined as Peter had been, but he wasn't rough. There was something quite special about him that she was going to have to ignore if she was to live at Labadette with any peace of mind.

'Now we start on the most difficult part of the climb,' Jean-Paul was saying. He was standing slightly above her, leaning forward, hand outstretched, a smile playing about his wide mouth.

Kelly looked up and blinked. This was no grassy slope that she could

amble up easily. She could brazen it out and pretend that it was nothing, but that hand he was offering her looked very tempting and she couldn't wait to have her own grasped in it.

'I'm not altogether helpless, you know,' she heard herself say, reaching out to him.

'I did not say that you were, but I would prefer to help you rather than to have you fall.'

It was good to feel the touch of a strong, masculine hand again. So good it was making her head spin slightly and her legs felt weak beneath her. Of course, that could have had something to do with the altitude.

'How high are we, Jean-Paul?' she asked.

'Oh, about a thousand metres. Not very high.'

'It sounds pretty high to me,' she panted, and wondered just how much farther they were going to have to climb before they reached the sheep.

'Not far now,' Jean-Paul said as if he

had read her mind. 'Listen.'

He stopped and gazed off to the right. Kelly could hear nothing. But then, as her breathing calmed down slightly, she heard the distant bleating of sheep and the clanging of the bells they wore around their necks.

Jean-Paul turned his eyes on her and kept them locked on her face, too long for comfort. She couldn't read his expression, but his eyes appeared to change, reflecting the mood of the sky above them as the wind blew the clouds across the face of the sun. Almost imperceptibly, his grip on her hand tightened. Kelly felt her throat constrict, and when she spoke her voice was thick and husky.

'Well, I don't know about you, but I'm ready for that picnic!'

His dark head jerked upwards and a quick smile creased his broad face. 'I know someone else who will be hungry by now, too.'

He meant Alex, but the boy was no longer anywhere to be seen. He had gone on without them, sure of the way and as nimble as a young gazelle. Kelly started to move forward, then stopped dead as a wolf whistle rang out from somewhere nearby.

'What the . . . ?' She looked around, taken completely off-guard, and heard the Basque laugh.

'A marmot, Kelly. There are many in these foothills. We have just disturbed one and he is warning his friends that danger is approaching.'

She laughed then, and he laughed with her. And those intoxicating brown eyes of his danced her way, lingering just long enough to disturb her equilibrium.

She liked the way he said her name with the accent on the second syllable rather than the usual first. He didn't often call her by her name and when he did it was almost as if it slipped out by accident.

Within minutes the ground flattened out and there were the sheep spread widely out before them on a great flat

117

plateau. A small lake of cobalt blue reflected them and the sky and the surrounding mountains like a mirror.

'Oh, how pretty!' Kelly breathed.

They had stopped walking and were standing close together. A tingling sensation tickled her palm and rose up her arm, into her chest as she realised he was still holding her hand.

'This is my special place,' he said and she wished foolishly that he would look at her with the same passion as he looked at the scenery. 'I used to come here with my grandfather when I was younger than Alex.'

Suddenly he let go her hand and the shimmering blues, greens and golds of the day went back to being ordinary.

★   ★   ★

Alex was sitting on a boulder a few feet away, kicking his heels and testing the strength of his trainers against the rough edges of the rock. He looked a little disgruntled and she guessed that

her presence was the cause. By now, he would normally be eating his bread and cheese lunch, drinking manfully from a bottle of spring water and enjoying an adult conversation on sheep, history and the arts with Jean-Paul. But today his mother was playing gooseberry.

'Shall we eat?' Kelly called out cheerily.

Jean-Paul took the backpack off and placed it on the ground next to a large flat rock. The rock made a good table and the ground around it was dry and mossy, so they could sit comfortably. Kelly unpacked the picnic of roast chicken, mixed salad, cheese and bread.

While she got things ready, Jean-Paul and Alex went about the business of checking the nearest group of sheep. They found a lame one and Kelly watched, fascinated, as Jean-Paul picked up the animal, turned it on its back and pulled on its injured hind leg. She heard a dull clunk. The beast got up immediately and walked blithely away, with Alex giving her a hefty pat on the rump.

'Food's ready!' Kelly called out to them and they turned hot faces in her direction. Jean-Paul raised a hand in acknowledgement, but he first took Alex to the edge of the lake where they washed their hands thoroughly and dried them on the coarse grass.

'Nothing serious,' Jean-Paul said, joining her. 'She must have fallen badly. Fortunately, it was only a dislocation and not a break. She's one of my best milk ewes.'

'Do you know them all personally?'

'Of course he does, Mum!' Alex piped up, eyeing the food hungrily.

'Not all of them.' The shepherd smiled indulgently at the boy. 'Kelly! What a feast! If I eat all this I won't want to work afterwards.'

It seemed like a rebuke, but his eyes were smiling at her gently.

'Can we start eating, Mum?' Alex was already installing himself cross-legged, grabbing a paper plate and deciding what to put on it.

'First you must drink something,

young man,' Jean-Paul insisted, handing Alex his bottle of water. 'You will be dehydrated. It is extra hot today and you are still new to this kind of weather. And your mother, too, *hein*?'

His eyebrows shot up when he saw her take out the bottle of wine. 'I thought . . . ' Kelly bit her lip and smiled shyly. 'Well, why not?'

He took the bottle from her and inspected the label. 'Cabernet Sauvignon! An excellent choice. You really do not want me to work this afternoon.'

'We don't have to drink it, if . . . '

He held out his hand for the bottle opener. 'You do not expect a Frenchman to turn down the opportunity of tasting a good wine,' he said with a boyish grin. 'Especially one who is more used to the vinegar served by Armand Soubirous.'

Alex was giving her a special, sanctimonious look as he bit into his chicken leg and got grease all over his flushed face. 'Wine! Yuck!'

'When you are a man, Alex,'

Jean-Paul said, tilting his glass so that the contents caught the sun and gleamed like a jewel, 'you will appreciate such things — wine, good food — beautiful women . . .'

'He's already started on the last one,' Kelly couldn't help saying, pulling a face at her son and being rewarded by a hearty laugh from Jean-Paul.

'Mum! Stop it!' Alex was furious, his eyes darting back and forward between Kelly and Jean-Paul.

'You have a girlfriend, Alex?' Jean-Paul asked, eyeing him playfully.

'No!'

'He has a crush,' Kelly supplied, 'on your fiancée.'

That produced a deep frown from Jean-Paul. 'My *fiancée*?' He really looked as if he didn't understand.

'Yes — you know, Yvette Bernardi.'

'Yvette?'

Alex got hastily to his feet and stomped off with his fists thrust deep into the pockets of his shorts, his narrow shoulders hunched. They watched him go and Kelly started to feel badly about upsetting him. She had joked about the situation, but in reality she had been selfish enough to do it because of her own curiosity. She wanted to know what the relationship was between the schoolteacher and the shepherd.

'Sorry about that,' she said, aware that Jean-Paul was watching her intently. 'I didn't realise he was so sensitive about it.'

'He is a child. He will get over it.' He watched Alex throwing stones and making ripples in the lake, his expression softening. 'Why do you call Yvette my fiancée? It is the second time you have done that.'

'Well, she is — isn't she?'

Jean-Paul gave her an unblinking stare, then a corner of his mouth lifted slightly and his eyes darkened and narrowed. 'No. Not at all.'

'But I — she — I mean . . . ' She gulped down a mouthful of wine. 'I'm sorry. It's really none of my business. I just thought . . . '

'Yvette and I have been friends — *only* friends — for a long time. I was engaged to her sister.'

'Yes — yes, I heard . . . '

'And did you also hear that I was responsible for Marie-Catherine's death? This is the story her family are fond of telling.'

Kelly stared down at her glass and swallowed hard. 'Yes.'

'And you believed it?'

She looked at him and shrugged. 'Actually, I didn't know what to think. Besides, I don't know the details — and since you're not in prison . . . '

He gave a short, mirthless chuckle.

'What did you think happened — that I had committed a *crime passionnel*? I assure you, it was not like that. There was no crime, despite all Delphine says. I was very young and . . . '

'Oh, please, Jean-Paul — don't feel obliged to tell me the details . . . '

'But I want to. I want you to know the truth.'

'All right . . . '

Her words trickled away in the breeze that wafted over them. He had fixed her in a gaze full of fire and it made her go hot and soft, like fondant chocolate melting in the sun. She drew her knees up and tucked her feet underneath her.

'As I said,' Jean-Paul continued, staring down into his glass as he twirled it around in his fingers, 'I was very young. A passionate young man still full of the innocence of youth, but with fire in my veins that would not be quenched. It is often like that for a man. They said I was wild. Perhaps they were right. Marie-Catherine was beautiful — and she knew how to use the power of that beauty.'

He hesitated and Kelly watched him, feeling very conscious of the fact that in talking to her like this, Jean-Paul was shedding his anonymity and making their relationship more intimate. They were no longer the Basque shepherd and the Englishwoman. She supposed they were halfway to becoming friends.

'What happened?' she prompted, hoping the story was not going to end there.

'I soon realised that I had made a mistake. It had been my body reacting, not my mind, not my heart. Suddenly I looked at her beauty and it did nothing for me but twist me inside. I knew I could never marry her. She was not the woman with whom I wanted to spend the rest of my life.

'I asked her to release me, but she refused. She became a little crazy, said some terrible things. I did not believe her when she said she would kill herself if I did not marry her. I went to the high pastures and when I came back down to the village they told me she was dead. She had taken an overdose of sleeping tablets.'

'How awful!' Kelly said, thinking that the girl must have been sick to do such a thing.

'I do not think she meant to kill herself. It was an attempt to get attention, to get sympathy, to force me into marrying her. Of course, her family blamed me.'

'But Yvette — her sister?'

'Yvette was jealous of Marie-Catherine. She always wanted what Marie-Catherine had. In this case, me. She has been trying to trap me into marriage ever since her sister died.' He looked up with a small smile and shrugged. 'Perhaps I am a fool to stay here, but it is my life.'

He lay back on his elbow, held his glass up to the sun, studied it, then his eyes drifted over to where she sat watching him. There was something in his expression that made her breath catch.

'The answer to your question, Kelly, is 'no'. There are no women in my life and have not been for a very long time. Too long.'

Then he sat up abruptly, drained his glass and turned his attention to the food spread out before them. 'Enough talk. Come, let's eat. I have the appetite of a horse.'

'Me, too,' she told him, smiling, and she was glad he couldn't see the turmoil he had caused inside her head. And the greater stirrings he had caused inside her heart.

First Kiss

Kelly occupied her time on the plateau that afternoon by sketching the lake and the sheep, putting man and boy in the foreground. Once or twice, as she looked up from her sketching, she caught Jean-Paul glancing her way. It gave her a ripple of excitement, which she found disturbing, but she quickly shrugged it off.

'You are a talented artist!'

His deep voice took her by surprise. She hadn't heard him approach.

'I hear you're pretty good yourself,' she told him.

'Oh, I am better with wood.'

'So Alex tells me. Perhaps you've missed your vocation.'

'Perhaps. Some dreams are more difficult to realise than others.'

The sky was darkening with black storm clouds appearing behind the mountains and sliding ominously over the land. The wind rose abruptly and cooling spots of rain fell on her sun-scorched arms and legs.

Jean-Paul called to Alex who ran towards them as the first rumble of thunder announced itself. Kelly felt the earth beneath her vibrate and a fork of lightning shot like a golden arrow behind the jagged crest of the Pic du Midi d'Ossau.

She hurriedly stuffed everything into her backpack. With a groan, she remembered that her waterproof was lying on her bed back at the house. It hadn't rained for five weeks or more.

'We must start back down the mountain,' Jean-Paul said as he joined her. 'Fortunately my work is finished for today.'

As before, he took charge of her backpack, though it was considerably lighter now with the food eaten and the bottles empty.

Alex was staring up at the sky, rain splotching him in huge droplets. 'Wow!

This is spectacular!'

Kelly laughed, thinking how he had changed in the last few weeks, for he had always been frightened of storms. Perhaps he was putting on the bravado for Jean-Paul's benefit. If that was the case, she was proud of him.

Jean-Paul pulled out his waterproof and offered it to Kelly, but she shook her head. 'No. It's Alex I'm worried about. He catches cold so easily.'

The poncho was duly draped about Alex's shoulders and went down to the ground, but he managed to walk without tripping over it.

'Come!' The order came from Jean-Paul, who was already striding out.

Kelly and Alex exchanged looks, Alex wrinkling his nose and grinning from beneath the shepherd's cape. Then they were running to catch up with him.

As they reached the steep shelf down from the plateau, Alex jumped down and ran on ahead, while Kelly hovered on the edge, wondering where to place her feet for the best. She was no mountain goat at the best of times, but right now she could hardly see through the driving rain, and the ground was made more hazardous with running water.

Jean-Paul turned, his hands coming up towards her. She caught her breath as he clasped her around the waist and lifted her down, their bodies grazing one another as she slowly descended to where he was standing.

She couldn't step back. There wasn't room. And Jean-Paul was showing no inclination to move. He was looking down at her, his eyes fathomless in the eerie light of the raging storm.

His arms slid around her, holding her tightly to him. She could feel his heart competing with her own, a non-too-steady thump vibrating between them. Glancing up, she saw an unexpected longing in his eyes.

'Jean-Paul!' she gasped, suddenly robbed of all her strength.

Rainwater ran in rivulets down her neck like cold fingers. She heard a soft, throaty groan, then he stepped back, releasing her abruptly.

He held out his hand and she slid hers into it. 'Come! Let us get you two back to the house.'

Kelly blinked damp eyelashes at him and gulped. She had momentarily forgotten about Alex, who was watching them broodingly from a few yards away.

Jean-Paul did not let go of her hand for the rest of the journey. Kelly was aware only of her churned-up emotions. An almost unbearable heat was rising from the soles of her feet to her cheeks and her head felt deliciously light.

Crazy! The word sang out in her brain over and over again. What was she doing contemplating a relationship with the local shepherd? He was a Frenchman, a Basque. He wore his hair long in a ponytail, for goodness' sake — she'd always hated that kind of thing. He belonged to an entirely different world.

'Nearly there!'

Jean-Paul's fingers tightened on hers and her whole being quivered. As they reached the valley, his pace quickened. He seemed to be dragging her along with him. Her feet hardly touched the ground.

The storm had abated slightly by the time they could see the lights of the village. They climbed the last part of the track together, Kelly's hand still in Jean-Paul's, Alex hanging on to her arm on the other side.

As they rounded the last bend Alex gave an excited whoop and shot forward. At first, Kelly didn't take it in, but then she saw a car in the drive and a light on inside the house. Her mouth dropped open and she stopped dead.

'You have visitors,' Jean-Paul noted softly.

'That's my brother-in-law's car,' she exclaimed.

They watched Alex disappear into the house, heard voices of welcome.

'You'd better come in, Jean-Paul,' she said with a long, dispirited sigh. 'At least they've lit a fire. You can dry off before . . . '

He put a hand on her shoulder and pulled her round to face him. 'I have my own fire here — ' he patted his chest ' — for you, Kelly!'

His mouth was seeking hers when her sister's voice from the open doorway of the house made them both jump.

'Hey, Kelly! What are you doing standing out there in this rain? Aren't you pleased to see us or something?'

'Sylvie! What a surprise!'

'I will leave you to your family,' Jean-Paul said huskily.

'Oh, no, Jean-Paul, please come and meet them.' Kelly shot him a wicked grin. 'If only to prove that you're not eighty years old and toothless.'

'Ah! In that case, I must defend my reputation.'

There was an army of small feet running down the path towards them, mindless of the rain that was still falling in a heavy curtain. 'Aunty Kelly! Aunty

Kelly! We came to see you in your new house!'

* * *

Sylvie and her husband and their four children sat side by side, crushed together on the long settee, all of them staring curiously at Jean-Paul.

'Well!' Sylvie smiled stiffly and looked embarrassed. 'Isn't this nice?'

'Terrible weather for this part of France!' Robert said gruffly as if it were somebody's fault that he'd found himself in the middle of a storm. 'Is it often like this here in the mountains?'

Kelly smiled at him patiently. 'No, but the storms can be fierce.'

'Does he speak English, Aunty Kelly?' Dora, the youngest of Sylvie's four offspring, was staring pointedly at Jean-Paul, who was steaming by the fire, having dried off as much as possible with a borrowed bath towel.

'Dora! Don't be rude! I'm sure *Monsieur* — er — Jean-Paul speaks

136

very good English.'

Jean-Paul frowned slightly, then shook his head with a smile. '*Je regrette.*'

'The children are learning French at school,' Sylvie enunciated carefully in a loud voice as if by sheer volume he would understand her meaning.

Kelly stared into the flames leaping up the chimney from the thick oak logs burning in the grate. The situation was ridiculous. There was absolutely no reason why they should all be embarrassed, but they were.

'It is all right, isn't it, Kelly?' Sylvie said. 'Staying here with you? You said there was plenty of room for us to visit and you sounded so down when I spoke to you last week . . . '

'Did I?'

'Well, I thought — why not? We're on holiday. Why not spend it in France with Kelly? The children were very excited, of course, at the prospect of seeing Alex again . . . '

Sylvie rambled on, but Kelly was only aware that she was sitting opposite

Jean-Paul and that his eyes were burning into her.

The outcome of the evening was soon decided for her. Alex, fresh out of the shower and sitting on the arm of Jean-Paul's chair, was suddenly overtaken by sleep. He slumped against Jean-Paul's broad shoulder, his head nodding on to the Frenchman's chest.

'There's one young man who needs to go to his bed,' laughed Sylvie.

Before Kelly could move, Jean-Paul was on his feet with Alex cradled in his arms like a baby. 'I will take him. Where is his room?'

'I — um — I'll show you.' Kelly jumped up and headed for the door with Jean-Paul, six pairs of eyes following her.

Alex didn't even wake up as Jean-Paul settled him on his bed and Kelly covered him over. They switched off the light and came out on to the landing.

'I must go,' Jean-Paul said softly.

'Yes,' she said, but allowed him to draw her into his arms.

'How long are they staying?'

Kelly pulled a face. 'They said a fortnight.'

'*Merde!*'

'I'm sorry, Jean-Paul. I didn't know they were coming. I — I certainly didn't plan the day to end this way.' She had been thinking more in terms of a candlelit supper and soft music.

'No, neither did I.' His hands were holding her face, his thumbs stroking her cheeks. His mouth found hers and his kiss was so sweet and so full of passion, she felt herself suffocating beneath it.

She pushed her hands firmly against his chest.

'I'm sorry, Jean-Paul,' she said shakily. 'But maybe it's for the best.'

'You are ashamed to be associated with me? I saw the way they looked — as if I were the hired help.'

'That's not true!'

'I think it is, Kelly. I think it was better when you did not look at me as if you wanted me. Then I knew my place.'

'How ridiculous!'

A soft click sounded from the floor below as a door opened and a yellow glow crept out into the hall.

'Kelly! Is it all right if I make the kids some hot chocolate?'

'Yes, of course, Sylvie!'

'How about you?'

'Not for me, thanks.'

'And your friend? Would he like anything?' Sylvie persisted.

'No, nothing, Sylvie. Jean-Paul's leaving now anyway.'

They went downstairs. Today had been a flash in the pan, Kelly was thinking, trying to be rational. Jean-Paul's kiss had happened in the heat of the moment — a chemistry type of thing that neither of them could explain.

At the door they stood like casual acquaintances once more. Jean-Paul did not touch her, did not look at her. He stared out into the silvery night with the rain falling softly, muting the colours.

'Tomorrow I will take the sheep

farther up the mountain to their summer grazing. I will stay with them. It is better that way.'

He gave a wistful little nod, then Kelly watched him walk away. She waited only a moment, then turned back into the hall just as Sylvie emerged from the kitchen with a tray full of steaming chocolate.

'Has your shepherd gone home, then?' she asked casually, but the expression on her face was not so casual.

'Yes, he's gone home.'

'Hmm. How long has he been ogling you like that?'

'What do you mean?' Kelly felt her face burst into flames. 'He doesn't ogle me.'

Sylvie smirked and headed for the sitting-room, saying over her shoulder, 'Of course he was ogling you. I fully expected him to pounce on you in front of us all.'

'What? Oh, don't be ridiculous, Sylvie!'

'The man was lusting after you, dear sister-in-law,' Robert frowned at her over his reading glasses. 'And if I didn't know you better I'd say you were lapping it up.'

'Really? Well, what if I was?'

'Now, now, you two!' Sylvie scolded, handing out the chocolate. 'If Kelly fancies a bit of rough to get her over Peter, good luck to her, I say.'

'He's not a bit of rough!' Kelly objected. 'Really, Sylvie, that's a hard judgement, just because he's not a city bloke with strings of letters after his name.'

'I'm sure he's very nice, Kelly — and quite intelligent — for a shepherd. But they are peasants, aren't they? I'd say that out here in the backwoods of France things are a bit more primitive than any of us can imagine.'

Kelly sighed loudly and tapped her toe against the fireguard, not trusting herself to speak.

'Are you going to marry the shepherd, Aunty Kelly?' Dora, the only girl in Sylvie's brood, wanted to know.

'No, I'm not!' Kelly snapped, then regretted her sudden anger. 'Oh, sweetheart, I'm sorry! I didn't mean to shout at you.'

The little girl's lips puckered and her eyes filled with tears. Her mother gathered her up in her arms and hugged her.

'Come on, Dora. Bedtime. Aunty Kelly didn't mean it.'

'I'm sorry!' Kelly whispered again, kissed her fingers and planted them on the child's forehead.

At midnight, Kelly and Sylvie were the only ones left staring at the dying embers of the fire. They hadn't spoken for a long time, but it was obvious that both of them had things to say. Finally, it was Sylvie who took the bull by the horns.

'You're not really contemplating getting involved with your Frenchman, are you?'

Kelly drew in breath and shrugged. 'Being sensible, I should say that it's far too soon to be making decisions one way or another . . . '

'But?'

'But I have a seriously disturbing feeling that's been growing in me ever since I clapped eyes on him.'

'It's got to be your hormones. I mean, let's face it, women like us just don't go around falling in love with men like that.'

'No, I suppose you're right, but . . . '

'Do you really like that pigtail thing he wears?'

'It's not a pigtail. It's a ponytail.' Kelly threw her hands in the air. 'Listen to me! I hate the things, but on him it looks fabulous!'

'Do you think it's too late for a nightcap? I think you need a good stiff drink and it's very bad to drink alone.'

'You're on,' Kelly said.

★   ★   ★

They took Alex to the airport the following Monday to see him off. 'I really don't want to go, Mum,' he said through gritted teeth.

'It's only two weeks, love, and your dad will be very disappointed if you don't go.'

She knew he wouldn't cry. He hadn't done that since his pet hamster died when he was four. Sometimes, she found his brave endurance far harder to cope with than childish tears.

'OK, but I won't enjoy it!'

'Well, even if you hate it, don't let it show or they'll be terribly hurt.'

'Mum, when you see Jean-Paul, will you remind him that he was supposed to be looking for a dog for me? Will you, please?'

'I don't think he'll forget, Alex,' she told him.

'But you'll remind him anyway, won't you?'

'Yes, all right, I'll remind him.' Then she grabbed hold of him and gave him a big hug, from which he emerged hot and embarrassed. 'Sorry, but I won't be seeing you for a fortnight. It's a mother's prerogative to hug her children, no matter how old they are.'

'It's all right. I don't mind.' He gave her a wan smile and looked nervously about him. He had never travelled alone before.

'Alex, you will be polite, won't you — I mean, in England — um — with your father and his — um — with Maggie.'

He nodded and chewed on his mouth.

'It won't be easy for any of you, but do your best,' she urged. 'I'm sure you'll be fine.'

'Huh!'

'OK, so fake it!'

He grinned at that and she hugged him again. This time he hugged her back and allowed kisses and hugs all round as the digitals on the airport clock showed that time was getting short.

★   ★   ★

Watching the plane taxi down the runway at Biarritz, Kelly felt her stomach lurch and she knew that was how Alex must be feeling too. She had been over-generous with his spending money and he had promised to buy her some of her favourite perfume to bring back with him.

Although he had grown and filled out considerably, he had still looked small and lost walking by the side of the flight attendant charged with his safekeeping. With a bit of luck, though, he would now forget his crush on the schoolteacher and develop a keen liking for hostesses of the air instead.

'Come on, Kelly!' Sylvie said, dragging her away as the plane climbed high in the sky and roared quickly out of sight. 'Stop fretting. Alex will be fine. Peter's meeting him at the airport, isn't he?'

'Yes, but I can't help worrying about how it'll be with his future stepmother. I know absolutely nothing about her except that she's far too old for Peter.'

'In that case, what was he doing walking out on you?'

'Peter never found the maternal thing he was constantly searching for in me. I just hope to goodness Alex doesn't take after him.'

'Well, you can change his diapers, but you can never change his genes. You just have to hope that he inherited the right bunch from the right parent.'

It was still early in the day, so they gave in to the pleas of the children to visit the beach at Biarritz. It was filled with bronzing beauties in bikinis and muscle-bound males flaunting themselves beside the surfing waves of the Atlantic.

'Kelly, are you listening to me?'

Kelly blinked at her sister, who hadn't stopped talking since they had left the airport and the constant drone of her voice was becoming monotonous.

'Sorry — what did you say?'

Sylvie frowned and sucked in her mouth, which made her look just like their mother.

'You were thinking about that shepherd again, weren't you?'

'Don't be silly,' Kelly lied. 'I was trying to remember if I had packed Alex's swimming trunks.'

They were, all six of them, lined up at the water's edge. Robert and the children were competing to see how far they could throw pebbles.

'I have to admit, Kelly, that the man really took me by surprise. I didn't expect him to be so — well, you know.'

'Gorgeous?'

'Hmm! I got quite a shock when he walked into the house. I swear, my temperature went sky high! Not that he's my type, but I can understand how you could feel attracted to all that power. He exudes it.'

Kelly went hot at the thought, but she managed a light laugh. 'You and your hormones, Sylvie!'

'Speaking of which . . . ' Sylvie's eyes drifted lovingly over to Robert, digging a hole in the wet sand and explaining the principles of irrigation to Dora. 'Number five is on his or her way.'

Motherhood, as Kelly well knew, was

Sylvie's great passion. She loved children.

'Does Robert know?' Kelly asked.

'Nobody knows yet. You're the first I've told. I'm just seeing how long it takes for Robert to cotton on. I was five months gone with Gary before he noticed. Do you think you'll see him again?' she added randomly.

'Who?'

'The big Basque bear.'

'I don't see how we can avoid one another. He's my closest neighbour.'

Kelly's heart sank at the thought of living so close to Jean-Paul and perhaps never getting close enough to touch him again. The magic that had built up between them had been severed and now he was going to be absent from the village for a long time. The relationship had been nothing but a passing novelty. Not at all realistic. Not a bit sensible, really.

'Well, you're a big girl now, Kelly, but I have to say this — I don't think he's right for you.'

'Oh? How can you say that? You and Robert hardly spoke two words to him.'

'Well, it's a little difficult when you don't speak the same language! What I'm trying to say is that you come from such different backgrounds. Can you honestly see yourself settling down to married life in a shepherd's hut in the middle of the Pyrenees?'

Kelly smoothed down the hairs on the back of her neck where they had risen of their own accord. She hadn't thought of any kind of permanency with Jean-Paul. She hadn't thought beyond that kiss and the secret longing it had caused, which refused to go away.

★　★　★

The heavy banging on the front door made Kelly jump. She was in the middle of making jam, stirring the fruity, sticky mess in the big pan on the stove, staring at the frothy red contents and trying to blank out her mind. As usual, it was full of romantic nonsense about Jean-Paul.

Before she could wipe her sticky fingers, the door rattled open, and Armand Soubirous appeared in her kitchen.

'*Alors*!' he said, his pink, jovial face taking a tour of the walls, his twinkling eyes poking nosily into every nook and cranny. 'I hope I do not disturb you, Madame Taylor, but I come as *maire* of Labadette to invite you to the *fête* on the fourteenth. The Committee tell me that you have not reserved a place.'

'Oh — er — I wasn't actually planning on going. I have my family visiting, you see, and . . . '

Actually, it was a poor excuse. She hadn't even told the family that there *was* a fête. She wasn't sure why, except that it was never easy to go to a social event without a partner. It wasn't just a meal. There would be music and dancing, and she loved to dance.

She refused to accept that the real reason for her reluctance was the fact that Jean-Paul might be there and all was confusion where he was concerned.

'But you must come, Madame Taylor!' Monsieur Soubirous was adamant. '*Everybody* comes to the *fête* of the fourteenth. Bring your family with you. You will be my guests.'

'Oh, but I couldn't let you . . . '

'That is my final word, *hein*! You will come.' It was an order rather than a question and she didn't dare back out now.

★   ★   ★

When Sylvie, Robert and the children came back from their day's outing to Paul, she told them about the invitation and they were obviously enthusiastic. They hadn't done all that much during their holiday apart from laze around, soaking up the sun. Robert wasn't the adventurous sort and Sylvie's ankles had swollen up badly with the heat. The children occupied themselves in the garden and the surrounding countryside. They had made friends, too, with the children in the village, Alex would be quite jealous when he found out.

Which reminded her, it was time for a phone call from him. In fact, he was late. At the beginning of his visit to his father, he had phoned her every two days with a report of his activities. However, four days had passed now without a word. She had tried ringing Peter's flat yesterday, but there had been no reply. The answering machine was obviously switched off. And there was no reply from his mobile either.

Although Kelly told herself repeatedly that there was absolutely nothing to worry about, she was, nevertheless, worried. Alex might be ill, or have had an accident, though surely someone would have informed her if there was a problem.

When the phone finally did ring, it was quite late in the evening and she was relieved to hear Alex's voice at the other end.

'Alex! Are you all right? Where have you been? You didn't ring and . . . '

'I'm all right, Mum!' he squawked back before she could go on. 'We've been staying at Maggie's. It's fantabulous! She's got all sorts of things like birds in cages and guess what — she's got a goat!'

Well, trust Maggie to have a goat. 'That's nice, dear. Where are you now?'

'Still there.' He was speaking in high-pitched italics and she realised that he was very excited. 'We're having a party. Maggie's grandchildren are here. They're great! They brought their pony with them and two dogs! Have you seen Jean-Paul yet?'

'Jean-Paul's still up on the mountain. You'll be able to speak to him yourself soon anyway, won't you?'

There was a short silence.

'Um — Dad wants to speak to you about that.'

'About what?' About Jean-Paul, did he mean? Well, Peter had a nerve if he thought he was still going to have any say in the running of her life.

'About . . . ' Alex cut off as Peter's

voice could be heard in the background. 'I've got to go, Mum. Here's Dad. 'Bye!'

'Oh — um — yes, 'bye, darling!'

'Kelly?'

'Hello, Peter. How's it going? Has he been behaving himself?'

'Yes, fine. Look, Maggie's got her family down here for the week and we thought — well, it was Alex's idea really — he'd like to stay on for another few days. That all right with you?'

Kelly felt her teeth grit together and when she spoke again she sounded a teeny bit strained. 'I suppose so. As long as — you know — er — Maggie doesn't feel it's an imposition.'

'Maggie? Gracious, no! She and Alex are really hitting it off. And now that her grandchildren have arrived — well, it seems like a good idea for him to stay on. You don't have any major objections, do you?'

'No, of course not.'

'By the way, what's this Alex tells me about you flirting with some scruffy shepherd he's palled up with? Jean something-or-other?'

Zap! Kelly felt the sarcasm hit her below the belt.

'He's called Jean-Paul and he's not scruffy — *and I don't flirt!*'

'Alex said you were. Something about a storm and this shepherd fellow being all over you. He was quite miffed about it all. Nose out of joint sort of thing. I gather he thought you were out to pinch his friend from him. How old is this Jean-Paul, then? The only shepherd I've come across was fat, filthy and in his dotage.'

'He's about the same age as you actually, Peter, and far from being fat or filthy. He's really quite a dish, if you must know. But he definitely was not 'all over' me.' Kelly's hackles were up. 'He just happened to lift me down a particularly hazardous bit of mountain and what Alex saw was . . . ' The memory of that moment came rushing back to give her palpitations.

'OK, OK, I believe you. You're hardly

likely to get hitched to that type anyway. I bet he smells of sheep and is infested with fleas. I've told Alex to stay away from him. He's picked up some really bad habits lately, like mopping his plate clean with a piece of bread. I ask you!'

'Well, it's quite in order to do that here in France *where we live*,' Kelly almost shouted down the phone and was tempted to mention a few of *his* bad habits, but that would almost certainly lead to a full-scale row. 'So, when's he coming back?'

'It's not certain yet. I'll have to look into flights and things and let you know. Probably in a week or so. In time for school, anyway.'

'School's not until September! You can't keep him until then.'

'We'll see. It might be best to send him to school here. At least it would keep him out of the way of local urchins and itinerant shepherds.'

'Jean-Paul is not itinerant.'

'OK, OK! Look, it's late. Let's

discuss things some other time.'

'There's nothing to discuss . . . ' But he had already gone, hanging up without another word. Kelly was left staring malevolently at the phone in her hand. It purred back at her like a fat, self-satisfied cat.

She was viciously thumping cushions back into shape in the sitting room when Sylvie wandered in, the usual mug of hot chocolate in her hand.

'I've just been speaking to Peter,' Kelly said and got an understanding grimace from her sister.

'I hope he's not tired of his toy-grandma and angling to come back.'

'Alex may be staying in London until September,' Kelly muttered, going a second round with the ill-fated cushions.

'Oh.'

'And Peter's talking about putting him into school there.'

'Oh.'

'Sylvie, don't just stand there saying

'oh' to everything. Don't you care? Don't you have an opinion on the matter?'

'Well, yes, but I don't like to interfere.' Sylvie curled up on the settee and spooned chocolate froth into her mouth. 'I always find that the person who influences a situation that has nothing to do with her invariably gets the blame. Therefore, I'm saying nothing.'

Kelly collapsed beside her with a loud sigh.

'Since when have you started taking a back seat?'

'Since I told you that you were a fool to marry Peter Taylor and you went ahead and did it anyway.'

Kelly picked up a cushion and cuddled it, seeking comfort from the gesture. The trouble was, the cushion didn't hug her back.

After a moment, she groaned and lifted her head. 'That night you arrived — it was the first time anything had sort of — well, sparked between me and Jean-Paul.'

'Sparked! When you two showed up at the gate, it was like bonfire night and Blackpool illuminations all rolled into one.'

Kelly sighed and groaned again. 'That's about how it felt, too.'

'And you've been tetchy ever since.'

'I'm sorry. Everything just hit me all at once. Jean-Paul . . . Alex . . . Peter . . . '

'I do think that the sooner you find yourself another man, the better you'll feel. Only you don't have to throw yourself at the first dishy male who walks your way. Find somebody better suited — somebody with brains and money and . . . why are you shaking your head?'

'I already did that once! It was the biggest mistake of my life.'

'So when is Monsieur Borotra coming down from his mountain?'

'Not until October, when he brings his sheep down for the winter.'

'That long, huh? Well, maybe you should take up rock-climbing.'

Kelly shuddered at the thought of

being completely alone with Jean-Paul on the top of a mountain with only the singing valley to listen to way down below them ... It was a nice dream, but only a dream.

She pushed it away behind her.

'I'm going to bed,' she said, feeling an uncharacteristic prick of tears behind her lids.

Jean-Paul Returns

On the fourteenth, the weather was hotter than ever. Kelly wandered down into the village in order to get away from her sister's fractious children, who were finally beginning to get bored and bothersome.

Red, blue and white bunting fluttered gaily in the breeze and there were the traditional long tables dressed with white paper cloths. A group of young musicians occupied a small bandstand where they were testing the amplifiers with ear-splitting results.

In one corner a fire was already burning and a whole sheep was turning on the spit. The menu for the night included barbecued mutton, 'kindly donated by Jean-Paul Borotra'. Kelly was almost glad that Alex wasn't there in case the sheep turned out to be one he recognised as a personal friend.

A marquee had been erected in another corner, which was where the rest of the meal was being prepared. Kelly spied Delphine Soubirous and her niece, Yvette. The latter looked flushed and more animated as she laughed and joked with two of the male caterers.

Kelly left them to it and called in at the *boulangerie* for the daily supply of bread. She was emerging back into the sunlight when Yvette appeared before her.

'*Bonjour, Madame Taylor,*' the school-teacher said formally and gave a bright smile that was a little tarnished around the edges. 'How are you? I do not see Alex in the village for a long time. He is well?'

'Yes, thank you. He's in England at the moment, with his father.'

'Ah! So, he will miss the *fête!* What a pity.'

'Yes, he was disappointed, but he's enjoying himself in London.'

'That is good. A boy needs to be with

his father.' Yvette tucked a wisp of hair behind her ear and her eyes narrowed coolly. 'My uncle tells me that you will be coming this evening.'

'Yes, he was kind enough to invite me.'

'You have visitors, no?'

'My sister and her family.'

'There is a man — your husband, I thought, but . . . '

'No, it's my brother-in-law.'

'Ah!' There was a strange light in the woman's eyes that Kelly couldn't make out. 'Well, you must excuse me. I have much to do.'

She sauntered off on long, slim legs, making heads turn. Where the men were appreciative, Kelly noticed that the women were less so. One or two followed her with a decidedly censoring look, giving their husbands the sharp edge of their tongue.

'Just like Marie-Catherine,' said a voice at her elbow and Kelly found Delphine Soubirous standing beside her.

'I'm sorry?'

'Yvette.' The woman's head nodded after her niece. 'So like her sister. It is no wonder the Basque likes her.'

'The Basque?' Kelly's tongue went dry inside her mouth.

'Jean-Paul Borotra. She tells me that he is coming down from the mountain. That is why she is so happy today. He would not come down from the mountain for anybody but Yvette. You will see, tonight, when they dance together.'

'I thought,' Kelly ventured, 'that they had split up.'

Delphine gave a low, wicked laugh. 'You believe that, do you? Never trust a Basque, *madame*.'

Never trust a Basque? Had Jean-Paul simply been playing with her, using her like a pawn in a game of chess in order to capture the queen? Perhaps she had been stupid to think that his feelings for her were genuine. Well, she would show him that she didn't care. She would go to the *fête* and she would laugh and dance as if he meant nothing to her. She had to do it, if only to save her own face.

Sylvie was waiting for her on the veranda when she got back with the bread.

'Hi! Did you see him? Your shepherd?'

Kelly frowned deeply. 'Jean-Paul?'

'Yes. He called in about half an hour ago. He seemed surprised to see us still here.'

So it was true. He was back.

'I didn't see him.'

'You look odd. Are you all right?'

Kelly ran some water into a glass and drank deeply.

'I'm fine. It's just so hot and I walked back a bit too quickly.' She forced a bright smile. 'Everything's getting underway in the village.'

'The kids are getting excited about staying up late. They'll probably all keel over before it's finished, but once in a while doesn't hurt, does it? You sure you're all right, Kelly?'

'I'm fine. Let's call everybody to the

table and get on with lunch, shall we?'

'Right! Then I can go and have my siesta and hope my ankles will go back to something like normal by tonight. I doubt I'll be doing any dancing though. You'll have to haul Robert around the floor if you can't find anything better than a French geriatric to trip the light fantastic with. That is, unless your shepherd . . . '

'No! I won't be dancing with him and you can stop calling him 'my' shepherd.'

'Oops! Did I touch a raw nerve?'

'Look, Sylvie,' she said, 'I went a bit mad and got carried away over John-Paul. It's called post-marriage-break-up syndrome. I should be grateful to you for arriving when you did. I was behaving like some kind of naïve idiot.'

'Oh, well, as long as you accept that, it's half the battle. Can we have lunch now, or do you want another therapy session?'

★ ★ ★

The hours dragged by with agonising slowness, but then at last it was time to get ready and go to the *fête*. Kelly pulled out a variety of outfits, tried them up against her, then slung them on the bed thinking that nothing she had was right.

In the end she settled for a turquoise top matched with a white skirt and low-heeled white sandals. She would have preferred high heels, but dancing in them or even standing in them for any length of time on concrete wouldn't be a good idea.

The band hadn't started by the time she arrived, but there was some taped music playing in the background and the little square was milling with people. It was all very jolly and looked like being a huge success with the evening warm and balmy and the sky clear and blue.

They had drinks at the makeshift bar, standing elbow to elbow with denim-clad men and rosy-cheeked women in floral skirts. Poor Robert was already looking bored, but the children were entering into the spirit of the open-air party. Somebody had produced party hats and streamers and spray cans of foam, so they were having a grand time under the watchful eye of some of the more elderly matrons of the village.

'Once the band starts up they'll be deaf for a week if they don't move away from that rostrum.' Sylvie laughed. 'Come on, let's install ourselves at a table.'

Although Kelly didn't eat much, the meal when it finally arrived at around ten o'clock was excellent. Dora fell asleep in a bowl of salad and was deftly removed to a safe place on a bench just behind them.

Just as Kelly was looking furtively around for a sight of Jean-Paul, Armand Soubirous materialised from nowhere and grabbed hold of her.

'You must dance, Madame Taylor!' he bellowed in her ear, marching her on to the floor.

Kelly gave a quivering smile while

she looked hastily over his shoulder for the daunting Delphine. However, Armand's wife was nowhere to be seen.

Clutched tightly to his bulky paunch she tried frantically to dodge his size twelves that insisted on trampling her toes.

When the music stopped he accompanied her graciously back to her seat, to startled glances from Sylvie who was getting ready to run to the loo if he decided to invite her on to the floor.

Kelly was surreptitiously massaging one bruised ankle when she saw a familiar figure entering the quadrangle. Far from looking happy, Yvette looked purple with rage. As she reached her aunt's table, where Delphine had reappeared and was talking with a group of women, she snapped out a few angry words and fell heavily into a vacant chair by her aunt's side.

In fascination, Kelly watched from a distance as the school-teacher grabbed a bottle of wine and poured herself a generous amount. She drank it in one go, then refilled the glass and sat there staring into space, her fingers grasped around a knife that she was tapping vigorously on the table in front of her.

Her aunt leaned towards her and said a few words. Yvette shook her head, threw down the knife then sank her face into her hands.

'Oh, dear!' Sylvie nudged Kelly. 'Do you see what's going on over there? Who is it?'

'That,' Kelly said tightly, 'is Yvette Bernardi — the school-teacher of this village.'

'Really? I wouldn't fancy her teaching my children. Has she had too much to drink, do you think? She looks awfully unhappy about something.'

'I don't know. She should be looking ecstatic right now, since Jean-Paul is supposed to be back and panting after her.'

'Ah!'

'Oh, don't you start with your 'ah'. You sound just like the French!'

Sylvie was smiling broadly and Kelly

felt like hitting her. She looked away just in time to see Jean-Paul walk in and all her senses were seized with a terrible tingling as her heart turned over and her mouth turned to ice.

'Robert,' she said, quickly turning to her brother-in-law, 'they're playing a waltz. Would you mind dancing with me?'

'What?'

'Dance with her, Robert,' Sylvie said, giving him a look.

'Oh, I really don't think I want to . . . '

'Please, Robert — just this one!' Kelly could see Jean-Paul standing with his back against the bar, leaning on it, his eyes dark and searching.

'I was just about to suggest we call it a day,' Robert was saying, looking plaintively at Sylvie, who pulled a face at him and sighed. 'Oh — um — yes, all right.'

He got up rather stiffly and hid a yawn behind his hand as they joined the dozen or so couples on the floor.

'What time do these things end, Kelly?' He glanced at his watch. 'It's after midnight and they haven't even served dessert!'

They waltzed slowly around the floor. Robert held her too rigidly so that her arms ached. As they passed the bar Kelly locked eyes with Jean-Paul for a brief moment. She couldn't hold it. His gaze was too intense, his eyes lit up with an inner fire.

The next time they came close to the bar, she noticed that he was no longer there. Twisting her head this way and that, she searched for him until her neck got stiff. A few minutes later the music stopped and she heard Robert's sigh of relief.

'Thank goodness. I'm beat.' The music started up again. 'Oh, no! Sorry, Kelly, but I think I'll take Sylvie and the kids home.'

'Oh, come on, Robert. Just this one last dance!'

'Sorry!' He walked away from her, leaving her standing there like a deserted island with couples floating around her, smiling sympathetically.

She sensed him before she heard him.

'Kelly, will you dance with me?'

She felt the touch of his hand on the small of her back, smelled the clean soapiness of him. She turned and was instantly enveloped in a pair of muscular arms.

For a long time they gazed at one another, not moving, though the music played on. Then he started to sway gently against her and she thought the music was fading, but it was just being replaced by the blood rushing to her ears.

'I didn't . . . ' She had to clear her throat and start again. 'I didn't know you were here.'

'Liar!'

'Yes, I'm sorry. I did see you, but . . . '

'I was late in arriving. I had — things to do. Important things.'

Something to do with Yvette Bernardi,

no doubt, she thought. What she said was: 'Shouldn't we be dancing?'

He laughed softly and his feet moved. She followed him, but she felt as if her body had frozen in time and space and no longer belonged to her. Then, gradually, she filled with a champagne burst of emotion as he whirled her expertly around the floor.

'You are beautiful this evening, Kelly.'

Oh, she wished he wouldn't say her name like that. It made her go all goosy. Her knees had already turned to jelly the minute he had taken hold of her and she hated her body for letting her down at the very time when she should be strong.

'I like your shirt,' she said, desperate that there should not be an uncomfortable silence between them. 'Is it new?'

'I was afraid you would not be here,' he said, ignoring the remark.

'What? And miss barbecued lamb? It was delicious, by the way. I take it you provided it? I've never tasted anything so good. The whole thing — the evening — well, it's been just . . . '

'You talk too much, Kelly.'

She looked up at him and her eyes clouded over. 'I don't know what else to do. I suppose you've seen Yvette. She's over there. I don't think she's very happy. You really shouldn't be dancing with me, you know, Jean-Paul. You should . . . '

'Be quiet!' His voice was soft, but the order was firm.

Kelly's mouth snapped shut and she melted against him. She didn't want to do it, not after all her plans to block him out of her life. No, she definitely didn't want to do this, but she couldn't help herself.

⋆   ⋆   ⋆

Suddenly there was a loud clack and a few sparks spewed out of one of the amplifiers. In an instant the whole place was plunged into darkness. Couples were groping their way about blindly.

Jean-Paul didn't move, except to put his hands on either side of Kelly's face and find her lips with his.

She gave in to the magic he was weaving all around her. People were laughing, lighting candles. Monsieur Soubirous was trying to make an announcement from the rostrum, but it was impossible to hear him above the rumpus.

'Come, Kelly.' Jean-Paul put an arm about her and dragged her through the crowd.

'Where are we going? I can't leave without . . . '

'Your family have already left. They know where you are.'

'I wish *I* did!' She pulled away from him as they neared the exit. 'Jean-Paul, are you playing a game with me or what?'

He stared at her, looking as confused as she felt. He started to say something, but got no further than opening his mouth before a shadow crossed them and someone rushed forward out of the throng. It was Yvette, with fists flailing — and in one of her fists she held a knife!

There were cries from a group of onlookers near enough to see what was happening. Kelly froze to the spot as if locked in some slow-motion film replay.

In one swift movement, Jean-Paul jumped between them and took the force of the knife. It clattered to the ground and Yvette screamed at him hysterically.

Numerous pairs of hands came from nowhere, grasping at Yvette, dragging her away. Jean-Paul hunched over slightly with a painful gasp, one hand pressed to a spreading red stain on his shirt.

'No!' he called out. 'Wait!'

'Jean-Paul — you're hurt!' Kelly touched his arm, but he held up a hand, shaking his head.

'It is nothing,' he said, then his attention was back on Yvette. 'I have something to say and I want you all to hear it. What you have just witnessed is the act of a sick woman. There has never been anything between Yvette Bernardi and me. *Never!* I was not her *amour*. I do not wish to be her *amour* — and I am no longer even her friend! She attacked Kelly because she is jealous. She would like to own me, but I am not the property of any woman. Now, please, take her away. She needs help.'

Armand Soubirous had pushed his way through and was gazing at the blood on Jean-Paul's shirt. 'Jean-Paul! Will you go to the police? Will you press charges? It is my wife's niece. She meant no harm. It was an accident.'

Jean-Paul stared at him, and then reached out and gripped Kelly's hand.

'There will be no police this time, but if she comes near me or Kelly once more, I'll see that she is locked up for a very long time.'

'Yes, Jean-Paul. You are very generous — very kind . . . '

Armand turned and took Yvette by the shoulders, shaking her briskly so that her head looked as if it were coming loose. 'Do you hear that, Yvette? Eh? We will have no more of this stupidity. Eh? Eh? No more! *Ca suffit, hein!*'

Jean-Paul drew Kelly gently away and they walked in silence until they reached the house, where Sylvie had left a light burning on the veranda. The house itself was in darkness.

'You'd better come in,' Kelly said. 'Let me look at that wound.'

But Jean-Paul had something more pressing in mind. He wrapped himself around her and his mouth fell on her neck, trailed up to her ear and then found her mouth.

'Now will you believe that there is no-one else?' he muttered against her lips. 'I have not been able to get you out of my mind, all this time alone up the mountain. This time, Kelly, you are not going to get away from me so easily . . . '

★ ★ ★

181

They did not go into the house. Instead, Jean-Paul took her to his cottage where Tricot greeted them joyfully for a minute or two before being silenced and sent to his kennel. Once inside, Jean-Paul would have kissed Kelly again, but she pushed him away, smiling at the hurt look in his warm, brown eyes.

'First let me do something about that wound,' she told him. 'Take off your shirt.'

She watched him as he pulled off the shirt and threw it to one side. The wound was nasty, but not too deep.

'Do you have any antiseptic? Something to bathe it with?' Kelly said.

He produced a bottle of clear liquid and some cotton wool out of a cupboard and gave it to her. 'The vet gave me this for Tricot when he tore his foot on a rusty nail.'

Kelly laughed. 'Well, I suppose it'll do.'

She dabbed the lotion on the wound, making him wince. Reaching out, she let her hands wander over his chest, feeling the pleasure of his hard muscles beneath her fingertips.

'I am nothing but a simple shepherd,' he said gruffly. 'You know that. I have no money, no fine things to offer you. But my heart is full of fine things and they are all yours.'

She slid her arms about him, kissed his chest, his shoulder, his throat. This was crazy, she kept telling herself, but she couldn't stop herself. She didn't want to stop.

As he kissed her eyelids and his thumb stroked her cheek, reawakening her senses, she tried to protest. 'Jean-Paul, I really must get back home. They'll be worried if I don't turn up.'

He smiled lazily as he continued to kiss her. Kelly felt mesmerised and completely unable to resist. But a frantic knocking on the door broke the spell. Jean-Paul frowned and went to answer it.

'Is Kelly here, please?'

She heard her sister's shaky voice and

felt a flash of irritation to think that Sylvie would have the nerve to come up here looking for her.

Jean-Paul stood back and Sylvie peered inside the cottage. Her face was flushed red with embarrassment, but her eyes were wide with worry. Kelly stepped forward, her hands planted firmly on her hips.

'Sylvie, if you've come here in the middle of the night to tell me that you don't approve . . . ' But she got no further.

'Kelly, it's Alex!' Sylvie said breathlessly.

'Alex? What about him?' Kelly felt a deep, churning premonition. 'What's happened?'

'I'm not sure. The phone was ringing when we arrived back. It was Peter.' Sylvie gulped. 'Alex has run away. Peter said they had a terrible time with him yesterday and now — well, he's gone missing. They've been looking for him for hours and now the police are involved — you know, just in case . . . '

Kelly's blood turned to ice and she began to shake. She jumped when Jean-Paul touched her shoulder and asked what the problem was. In a shaky voice, she gave him a quick translation.

'Something must have happened to make him unhappy,' Jean-Paul said. 'He should not have gone to England. He never wanted to go.'

'Yes, I know,' Kelly said, too numb to feel anything but anxiety. 'Look, I'm sorry about this, but I must go to London. I've got to be there for him.'

'Yes, of course.' Jean-Paul nodded solemnly, then he leaned forward and kissed her firmly on the mouth, his eyes dark. 'You will come back, yes?'

She nodded. 'Yes.' She grabbed his hand and squeezed it, then she was running back down the hill with Sylvie.

'We're all booked on the same flight back home,' Sylvie said as she hurried along at her side. 'Robert's already packing our things. We can go back home today just as well as tomorrow. There's no problem there.'

'Oh, Sylvie — what if they don't find him? What if something terrible has happened to him? I'll never forgive myself.'

Poor, Confused Alex

The plane descended through thick grey clouds into a grey London huddled under a blanket of rain. It felt cold after the south-west of France and Kelly shivered convulsively as she stood in the busy arrivals lounge and looked about her for Peter.

Fifteen agonising minutes went by. Kelly shifted her weight from one foot to the other and hoped she didn't look as wretched as she felt.

'You must be Kelly!'

She turned at the sound of her name. The deep, gravelly female voice belonged to a tall, elegantly-clad woman who was strikingly handsome rather than beautiful.

'Yes, I'm Kelly,' she said and the woman held out her hand in greeting.

'I'm Maggie Malloy.'

'Oh! I — I didn't expect . . . Where's Peter?'

'We thought it best that he stay behind and wait for Alex.'

'They've found him?' Kelly asked, her voice wobbling precariously.

The woman smiled kindly and nodded. 'Yes.'

'Thank God!'

Peter's new partner put an arm around Kelly's shoulders and gave her a motherly hug, then urged her to walk with her towards the exit doors.

'Come on. I'm sure he'll be more than glad to see you.'

'Where was he?'

'A local farmer in Sussex found him in his barn, asleep in the hay.'

'In Sussex!'

'Apparently he'd hitched a ride that far, thinking he could get back to France, then he changed his mind and didn't know what to do.'

Once installed in Maggie's luxurious silver grey Saab, Kelly started to relax.

Her eyes slid slyly over to the woman next to her.

Maggie saw her looking and gave a throaty chuckle.

'I'm quite happy to answer questions,' she said, negotiating her way through the heavy early-evening traffic around the airport.

'I'm sorry. I didn't mean to be rude, but you're not what I expected. You certainly don't look like anybody's grandmother.'

Maggie threw her handsome head back and laughed loudly.

'I don't *feel* like a grandmother. I got married young, had my children quick and left them to their own devices as soon as they showed signs of knowing what they were doing. My husband died fifteen years ago. When I met Peter it was like a spring breeze blowing through my life, but I never at any time expected anything to come of our relationship.'

'You — um — you were . . . ?'

'Purely business for a while. Then . . . '

She lifted her shoulders and a private smile spread widely over her oval face. 'A touch of magic. Lightning striking just at the right time.'

Magic. Kelly swallowed hard. She had never really known any magic with Peter. That had been one of their problems. Perhaps their greatest problem. Nothing ever had — sparked. Not the way it did with Jean-Paul.

She stared blindly out at the road as the Saab ate up mile after mile, her head reeling with so many unasked questions.

'Kelly, I hope there are going to be no bad feelings between us.' Maggie glanced at her, eyes shimmering in the lowering sun. 'I do think it's important — for Alex — that we all get along.'

Kelly smiled. Despite herself, she found there was something very like-able about this woman and there was a lot in what she said.

'It's all right, Maggie. I don't blame you. Peter and I had drifted apart long before you came on the scene. We were never right for each other in the first place.'

'That's what Peter says. But you have a great son.'

Kelly groaned. 'So great he pulls this stupid trick of running away and worrying me to death.'

'If it's any consolation, Peter was worried, too.'

'That does surprise me. Peter never took to fatherhood. He did what he had to do, mostly under duress. I only talked Alex into coming over to London because I thought he was in danger of becoming a mother's boy.'

'Aha! I don't think you have to worry about that. Who's this person called Jean-Paul he talks about constantly?'

'Jean-Paul?' Kelly's throat had contracted the instant his name was mentioned. 'He's a friend — a neighbour.'

'Hmm. Alex thinks he's the bee's knees.' Another flash of green eyes came Kelly's way. 'Are you — close?'

Kelly hesitated and felt her cheeks

flare. 'Not exactly, but . . . '

'Ah, I thought as much. You have a very perceptive son, Kelly. He guessed there was something between you and this Frenchman. Poor Alex. He's all mixed up because he's not old enough yet to understand. He feels that everybody in his life is being taken from him.'

'Is that why he ran away?'

There was a very noticeable pause.

'Who knows? Anyway, we're nearly there. You can discuss all that with Peter. I promise I won't interfere.'

The house was a large, Georgian red-brick manor set back from the road behind high iron railings. Two red setters loped up to the car, yelping madly as Maggie parked in front of the double garage. Kelly could see that Peter would be impressed by the place, though he wouldn't be too much at ease with the dogs bounding around him.

The door opened as the car's engine faded. Kelly got out, instantly recognising

ever so slightly. 'No.'

'OK.' Kelly sat down beside him. 'That means it's all *my* fault, so it's a jolly good job I came over to see you, because otherwise I wouldn't be able to speak up in my own defence.'

The small shoulders rose and fell. 'Don't know.'

'What don't you know?'

'Everything!' Alex flashed her a look and she saw his eyes well up with tears, which he dashed away with his knuckles before he stared off into space again.

Kelly looked across at Peter, who was standing in classic pose with one arm resting along the high marble mantel-piece. She wished he hadn't stayed, sure that she could have dealt better with the situation without his heavy presence.

At that moment, there was a rattle of crockery and Maggie came in carrying a silver tea-tray. 'I'm sure you're ready for a cuppa, Kelly.'

'Yes, I am, thank you.'

'Can I go to bed?' Alex was on his feet and halfway to the door, not looking at anybody.

'Alex!' Peter shouted after him sharply, and the boy halted in his tracks but kept his back to the room. 'You'll stay here and give your mother — give us *all*, an explanation for your behaviour today.'

'No, Peter! Please . . . ' Kelly pleaded with her eyes. 'Let him go. It's all right, Alex. You go to bed. We can talk in the morning.'

Peter started to argue and Kelly was suddenly reminded of the years of stress he had caused by his bloody-mindedness.

'Peter.' Maggie put the tray down and touched Peter's rigid arm. 'Kelly's right. Let the boy be. He's had quite enough for one day, and so have we.'

'Bah!' Peter brayed like a discontented mule, but he said no more on the subject and Alex disappeared. They listened to his bare feet flapping through the hall, then the gentle thump of them as he ran up the stairs, followed by the click of a door.

'Kelly, you're more than welcome to stay the night,' Maggie said kindly. 'The children and the grandchildren have gone home, so there are plenty of spare beds.'

'Oh, really, I can't . . . '

'Nonsense! You need to be close to Alex.'

'Well, yes, but . . . '

'Oh, for Pete's sake, Kelly, stay!' Peter ground out.

There was an awkward silence when all Kelly could hear was the hollow ticking of the grandfather clock from the hall and the dainty chink of Maggie's cup on her saucer as she sipped her tea.

'Why don't you go for a walk, dear?' Maggie suggested finally to Peter. 'Take the dogs. They'll enjoy the extra exercise. It'll give Kelly and I a chance to become better acquainted.'

Peter had his hands stuffed deeply into his trouser pockets and he was wearing his 'little boy in a sulk' scowl. Kelly waited with interest to see if he would take up the challenge of walking the dogs. Maybe he had developed a love for animals along with his new relationship.

'I don't want to go for a walk!' he snapped. *'Flippin' dogs!'*

No, he hadn't changed. Still the same person as before — anti-animal, anti-people most of the time. It was a wonder he hadn't become a hermit living in total seclusion by now.

He made a small, exasperated sound and picked up a folded newspaper from the coffee table. 'I'll go and read in the library. Give me a call when dinner's ready.'

★   ★   ★

Maggie waited until he had left the room, closing the door with an impatient snap behind him, then she turned to Kelly and smiled. 'Men! They're all children at heart, aren't they?'

'Well, I know Peter is.' Kelly smiled

back. 'I haven't really known any other men to draw comparisons.'

'Take my word for it, my dear. They never like being told what to do, but quite honestly, it's the only way to get them going in the right direction.'

'Are you really going to marry him?' Kelly didn't quite know why she asked the question.

'Is that what he told you?'

'Well — um — no. When he said he'd found somebody else, I suppose I automatically assumed that he'd be getting married. I was wrong, wasn't I?'

'Yes, you were. Why? Do you want him back?'

'No!'

Maggie laughed softly. 'Well, that was positive enough anyway! Now, let's talk about your son.'

Kelly jerked upright at that. 'You definitely can't have *him*!'

Maggie was shaking her head and still laughing, half to herself.

'Much as I think Alex is adorable, I've had my fill of husbands and children. Short visits are about as much as I can stand at my age — which is sixty, by the way, just in case you're wondering.'

'Oh, I wasn't — really!' Kelly lied, amazed that a woman old enough to be her mother could look that good.

'The thing is, Kelly, Alex is feeling pulled in too many directions. His emotions are all mixed up. He doesn't want to stay here, but he doesn't want to go back to France either.

'He feels things strongly, only he doesn't understand exactly what it is he's feeling. All he knows is that the people he loves all seem to love somebody else and he feels locked out, so he doesn't know which way to turn. I think that's why he ran away. Maybe there was some crazy idea that if you and Peter were worried enough over him you'd get back together and at least he'd know where he stood. It works in films. I'm not so sure about real life.'

'Peter wants to put him in boarding-school,' Kelly said miserably.

'Yes, I know, but I don't think that would do anything other than confirm what Alex feels right now.'

'That nobody loves him, you mean?'

Maggie patted her hand and re-filled her cup with tea.

'It's none of my business, I know, but I think Alex would be better off with you. Peter should never have been a father. He doesn't like children any more than he likes animals.'

Kelly smiled at the older woman over the rim of her cup. Maggie was right, of course, but Alex still needed the firm hand of a man in his life. A man he could look up to as well as love.

Jean-Paul was perhaps that kind of man, but just how permanent was he planning to be in their lives? She had never forgotten his words at the fête, issued in front of the whole village. *'I am not the property of any woman.'*

Return To France

In the end, Kelly stayed a week in Maggie's house with Alex, while Peter went back to his London flat, which was too small to share even with a ten-year-old. It wasn't practical for him to commute to the office from Weybourne.

There had been a lot of discussion, with Alex present, and they had agreed that Peter should take some holiday time and go back with them to France. It was a short-term compromise that they hoped would work. However, the very thought of living again under the same roof as Peter was hardly ideal from Kelly's point of view.

If Maggie didn't like the idea, she kept quiet about it and drove them all to the airport the following weekend as if they were old family friends.

Their flight was called after a short

delay that seemed to last for ever. Kelly started off towards the gate, feeling strange giving her husband's 'girlfriend' a cheery wave of goodbye, but it was nevertheless sincere.

When they touched down in Paris, the day was hot and hazy with pollution as thick as smog. Kelly and Alex waited in the hired Ford Focus while Peter bought some road maps.

'Is there a radio?' Alex said, hanging over the back of Kelly's seat.

'Yes, but it'll be in French and you know what your dad's like. He hates chatter of any kind while he's driving.'

'Uh-huh. Especially in French.'

Alex sucked in his cheeks and stared out through the front windscreen, making bird noises.

'Alex, I hope you appreciate all this,' Kelly said, seizing the opportunity to have a few words. 'You haven't behaved like I would expect you to behave. We should have given you a good thrashing for running off like that and making us worry.'

'Sorry.'

He slumped back into his seat and she swivelled around so they could talk face to face. His blue eyes held a challenge she wasn't at all sure about, but she had held her peace for long enough.

'We didn't get too angry because we figured you had some problems that need sorting out.'

He shrugged and stared down at his fingers.

'You do understand about divorce, don't you, Alex? I mean, I went to great lengths to explain it to you. Your father and I no longer want to live together.'

'Yes, I know that!'

'Your father is going to live in London and I'm going to live in France. You chose to stay with me, for which I was very glad. But what on earth are you trying to do now?'

Another shrug.

'If you think you're going to persuade us to get back together, Alex, it's a very big mistake. Is that what you have in mind?'

His head lifted and his eyes swept her face and went on to stare at a family of five who were piling into the car next door.

'I just want — I don't know! I just thought — if we were all together — you and me and Dad and . . . ' He blew out a soft current of air and started nibbling at his nails.

'You never liked it when the three of us were together before. What's so different now?' She suddenly did a mental double take. 'Alex, has this anything to do with Jean-Paul?'

His face looked hot. Alex took after her in that department. They were both very good at blushing.

'Jean-Paul was *my* friend,' he said solemnly. 'But that day on the mountain, you — he . . . ' His mouth twisted and she thought for one awful moment he was going to cry.

'Alex, you can't own people like that, like a pen or a book. People are allowed to have more than one friend. *You've got* more than one friend. Half the children in the village are your friends, and now you've got Maggie's grandchildren. I'm sure you've agreed to exchange letters with them and see them when you go back to England in the holidays. Haven't you?'

'Yes.'

'Yes! So, Jean-Paul is allowed to have more than you for a friend.'

'Like you?'

'Yes, like me! Of course! Why not?'

'That day on the mountain — I saw him kiss you and you let him do it.'

Kelly sighed. So that was it.

'It was adult stuff, Alex. That kind of thing — it happens between grown-ups. It's called mutual attraction.'

'Like love?'

'It can lead to love, if you're lucky.' Kelly smiled and hoped it might be catching, but Alex still looked very morose. 'You'll find out when you're older. In the meantime, you have to accept that no matter what happens between Jean-Paul and me — he's still your friend.'

The car door clicked open and Peter got in, his hands full of maps. He passed them over to her, indicating the one that was already open and pointing out the route they were to take.

'Right, let's get going. Alex, seat belt!'

A few miles later Peter was already shouting impatiently at Kelly because of her poor navigational skills. She had never been much good at it, but today her head was full of more pressing things than getting from Paris to Labadette.

They stopped for the night in the picturesque village just outside Poitiers. Peter was getting more and more tetchy and claimed he was too tired to drive farther. He booked a couple of rooms in a bed and breakfast place, then they had dinner at an *auberge*.

After a pleasant enough meal, they walked slowly back to the hotel because it was a beautiful evening and still quite early. Alex seemed to be a lot more settled now that he was back on French soil.

'Is there a telly in the hotel room?' he wanted to know.

'Yes,' Peter told him, 'but I don't want you staying up half the night.'

'Can we go back to the hotel now?'

'Oh, Alex,' Kelly chided. 'It's far too nice out here in the fresh air to rush back and watch television!'

'Oh, please! Can I?'

Peter dug in his pocket and produced a key with a number on.

'OK. That's your room. Off you go, but don't be a nuisance, and lights out at the usual time, eh?'

Alex was so pleased at being given some autonomy he forgot to argue about the lights-out bit. He grabbed the key and raced off.

Alex had a room to himself, Kelly discovered later, and she was apparently expected to share with Peter. She was unhappy about the arrangement and let him know it.

'It wouldn't have looked right,' he

argued, bumping the door shut behind him. 'Besides, we got the only two rooms they had left.'

'There must have been other places to try! Or you could have shared with Alex.'

'And waken him up when I got in? Besides, what's wrong with this?'

Kelly glowered at him angrily. 'It's a double bed!' she pointed out.

'So? We shared the same bed for twelve years.'

'Peter! We're not a couple any more.'

He sat down heavily on the bed and the springs twanged. 'It's a big bed — but I'll sleep on the floor if you're that bothered. See if I care.'

'I don't believe this, Peter. I really don't!'

Pulling the covers off the bed and finding extra blankets in the wardrobe, she marched into the bathroom and locked the door behind her.

She threw everything into the bath, which was large and old-fashioned and she hoped the taps didn't drip. It was just big enough for her to lie reasonably stretched out and although it wasn't as soft as the bed it was all her own.

★ ★ ★

'What's wrong with your neck, Mum?' Alex asked her after breakfast.

'I must have slept in a draught,' she told him, rubbing her stiff neck and giving Peter a chilling look.

Kelly insisted on Alex sitting in the front beside his father for the rest of the journey. She said it would be good experience for him, reading maps. Peter objected mildly, but didn't carry the argument too far. As it happened, Alex proved himself to be better than she was, so she was quite happy to let him do it.

She must have dropped off to sleep for the last hour or two, because suddenly they were there, bumping up the track to the house and Peter was commenting on how disgustingly rustic the place was.

'You can't really be planning to stay here,' he said, unable to keep the sniffiness out of his voice.

'It'll look really good when I get round to having it done up,' she assured him. 'It's got amazing potential. Anyway, I like it and that's all that matters.'

As they got out of the car, Kelly couldn't prevent her eyes from straying up the hill to Jean-Paul's cottage.

'Jean-Paul lives there,' Alex pointed, and Kelly's stomach did a backward flip.

Peter followed the direction of his pointing finger. 'Does he really? I wouldn't have thought anybody could live in a ramshackle old shoebox like that.'

'I certainly don't suppose you could,' Kelly said, fishing for her key. 'Come on, I could murder a cup of tea.'

The house felt cold with being shut up for a week and there was a faint smell of damp. The hot summer sun hadn't been able to penetrate the two-foot-thick stone walls and she saw Peter shiver as he came in and looked around him with obvious disdain.

'I'm gradually getting it into shape,' Kelly told him defensively. 'Sit down. I'll light a fire. It'll air the place off.'

He didn't sit down, but stood there in the middle of the room, a fish out of water, watching her as she bustled about, fetching sticks and logs. She noticed he didn't offer to help.

'Why couldn't you buy a house with central heating like the last one? I still don't understand why you felt it necessary to move in the first place.'

'In the first place?' She struck a match and put it to the rolled up paper beneath the sticks. It caught immediately and there was a welcoming crackle and a smell of sulphur and wood smoke. 'I hated that house. Anyway, I thought it would be good for Alex to experience life in the country.'

Peter turned away from her. 'Oh, Kelly! What are we doing?'

Kelly looked up to check where Alex was, but he had wandered off somewhere. It was safe to speak.

'I'll tell you what we're doing, Peter. You are staying with us for a few days at your son's request. It seems only fair, since we forced an English holiday on him. At the end of those few days you are returning to England — to Maggie.'

'Come back with me, Kelly — please!'

The flames were licking their way up the wide chimney and Kelly held her hands out to them, enjoying the warmth. She cast a disbelieving glance over her shoulder and saw the raw pain in Peter's face.

'Go back to England? Do you mean you want us to get back together again — as husband and wife? A family unit?'

'Yes. We can start again. Alex can go to boarding-school. You can find a job — or stay at home. Whatever you want, Kelly, I wouldn't have come here if I hadn't thought there was a chance.'

She straightened up and faced him. 'Peter, listen to me. There isn't a chance in a million. I don't want you, it's as simple as that.'

'Is there someone else?'

She hesitated. 'Perhaps,' she said, knowing in her heart that it was too soon to give a definite answer. 'I hope so. But even if there wasn't — I still wouldn't want you back. I'm sorry, Peter, but if you hadn't left me for Maggie, I was going to ask you to leave anyway. Do I make myself clear?'

He heaved a raucous sigh and rubbed a weary hand over his eyes. 'You'd better show me where I'm sleeping then.'

Kelly bit her lip, feeling unexpectedly awash with pity. He looked so pathetic standing there, a forty-year-old little boy not knowing which way to turn.

'It's the room on the left at the top of the stairs. I think you'll find it comfortable enough. You're next door to Alex.'

He nodded and picked up his suitcase, walking dejectedly out of the room.

The knock on the door took her by surprise. She didn't often get visitors. For a moment her heart lifted, thinking it might be Jean-Paul, but it was a false hope. He was probably sitting under the stars at two thousand metres counting his sheep.

'Remi!' The shepherd was the last person she had expected to see.

The old man dragged off his black beret, held it over his heart and gave her a toothless grin. 'Madame! I see your light and the car and I say to myself, the Englishwoman has come back. I will tell Jean-Paul. He will be pleased.'

'Come in, Remi. Sit down. Would you like a drink?'

'Oh, yes! You are very kind. The boy is here? Ah!'

The boy in question had just come into the room and the two exchanged amicable grins.

Kelly put a generous whisky in the gnarled old hand.

'How is . . . ?' Kelly had to clear her throat and start again. 'How is Jean-Paul?'

Remi pulled a long earlobe and smacked his lips over the taste of the whisky.

'He is on the mountain.' One finger pointed to the ceiling. 'I take him supplies yesterday. He says he is fine, but I know Jean-Paul.' The finger now pointed to the puffy bag under one eye and he pulled it down, revealing a bloodshot eyeball. 'There is something wrong.'

'What is it? Is he ill?' Kelly's heart thumped.

'Ill? No!' The finger waggled at her, back and forth, then he tapped his temple. 'Not ill, but something bothers him.'

'How's Tricot?' Alex wanted to know, but the old man's reply was stemmed by the unexpected appearance of Peter, dressed only in a royal blue dressing-gown and a towel draped around his neck.

'Do we all use the same bathroom, and is that bottle of orange stuff shampoo or what? Oh!' He blinked at Remi, who stood up and blinked back. 'I suppose this is your shepherd friend, Jean-Paul?'

Kelly opened her mouth to put him right, but Alex got there first with a loud laugh. 'No, Dad. This is Remi. He works with Jean-Paul sometimes. Remi, this is my father. He's come to stay.'

'Well, not stay, exactly . . . ' Kelly started to say, but the old shepherd had gone to shake hands with Peter, and because he was quite deaf he didn't hear her.

'I'll go and put the kettle on. There must be something in the freezer we can eat.' She touched Remi's shoulder and raised her voice. 'Remi, will you eat with us?'

'For Pete's sake, Kelly!' Peter objected, unable to hide his disgust. 'Do we have to sit down with the peasants because we live in the country?'

She flashed him a warning look, relieved that the old man would have no idea what was being said. Remi shook his head and swallowed back his whisky.

'*Merci, non!* It is good to see you, *madame*. Jean-Paul will be happy too.'

217

'Thank you, Remi.'

She went with him to the door, where he stuck his beret back on his bald pate and nodded a few times.

'Ah! I have news!' It came out as an afterthought and he leaned towards her conspiratorially. 'The school-teacher, Yvette.'

Kelly's stomach did a complete turn. 'What about her?'

'She has gone! Pouff! Like a feather on the wind. That stupid aunt of hers, Delphine Soubirous, is telling everybody that she has found another job somewhere at the other side of France. The whole of Labadette is talking about it. The truth is that she has gone into a hospital for the sick in the head. Ach, the whole family is mad.' He gave his temple a meaningful tap. 'I will tell Jean-Paul you say hello.'

'Yes — please do, Remi — and thank you.'

He ambled stiffly back down the track, his back bent, his legs bowed beneath the weight of his years.

'What a detestable old codger!' Peter

said as she went back inside. 'I don't think it's advisable to invite people like that into your home, Kelly.'

'Oh, Dad!' Alex screwed up his face and looked to Kelly for support.

'Remi's an old countryman and he's worked his fingers to the bone all his life,' Kelly protested stoutly. 'If I had to choose between people like him and the people you socialise with, I know which I would choose.'

'You amaze me, Kelly.'

'Just recently, Peter, I've amazed myself. Now, what were you saying about the bathroom?'

★ ★ ★

The next few days put a strain on Kelly, but she supposed it was the same for Peter. To give him his due, after the first few tense hours, he seemed to relax. Alex couldn't persuade him to go for country rambles, however, and had to make do with visiting historic monuments and museums.

Just before Peter was due to return to England he surprised Kelly by suggesting they all spend the day at Pau and eat out at a restaurant. Alex pulled a face, but was rewarded for his patience by being taken around the medieval *chateau*, even gazing in awe at the gigantic tapestries that adorned the walls.

As they were heading back to the car-park, they stopped to look in a small art gallery just off the *Promenade des Anglais*. Kelly's eye was caught by two attractive woodcarvings. Unlike the imitation wood plaques found in the tourist shops, these were genuine and depicted sheep, a shepherd and a cheese-making scene.

The lady in charge of the gallery was all aflutter in the hope of making a sale. She homed in on Kelly, while Peter stood back resignedly.

'Ah, *madame*, this is quite the most exquisite work, don't you think? Look at the quality. This artist is one of our best sellers, but he does not provide us with enough. Such a pity.'

Kelly was turning over one of the wooden plaques in her hands, feeling the satiny smoothness of the wood.

'I do like this one. Who is the artist? I don't see a name.'

The woman directed a long fingernail to a minute indentation of initials in one corner, almost hidden among a clump of carved grasses. J-P.B. No! Surely, it couldn't be . . .

'Jean-Paul Borotra, *madame*. It is hard to believe that this man who executes such delicate work is nothing more than a shepherd here in the Pyrenees. A simple working man, and he can turn out such beauty as this.'

'Alex!' Kelly called out. 'Alex, come and see. Jean-Paul did this.'

'Really?'

Alex showed little interest and walked away as Peter came and took the plaque, inspecting it with the eye of a connoisseur.

'That shepherd fellow did this, you say? Hmm.'

221

'I'm going to buy it,' Kelly decided, fumbling in her bag for her cheque-book. She looked apologetically at the woman. 'I wish I could buy both of them. They're really lovely, but . . . '

'It would be a pity not to, *madame*. They are really collectors' pieces.'

'He makes furniture too,' Kelly suddenly remembered. 'Did you know that?'

The woman's fine-pencilled eyebrows twitched and she pursed her lips.

'No, I didn't. We have another shop, much bigger than this one, in Biarritz. Perhaps I will have a word with Monsieur Borotra the next time he comes in. These two carvings are all we have left of his work. Such a pity to separate them. They go together so well.'

Kelly had to agree. It was a pity to split the two plaques up, but they were expensive and she had to be careful these days. There was so much work needed to renovate the house and her old car would have to be replaced soon, among other things.

She glanced up at Peter, who now had both plaques in his hands.

'All right, all right — I'll pay for them both.' He produced his credit card. 'Call it a leaving present.'

Outside, it was clouding over and starting to rain. Kelly clutched her precious parcel, hugging it as if it was Jean-Paul himself she had in there.

'That was very generous of you, Peter. Thank you.'

He shrugged and gave her a sad little smile.

'You're welcome,' he said. 'Something to remember me by, I hope.'

Now she felt guilty. It was ironic that the last thing Peter should have bought her was something made by Jean-Paul.

Down From
The Mountain

When the first day of September arrived the weather was again beautiful, but not quite as hot as it had been during July and August. They could breathe again and the tiled floors in the house no longer sweated and got greasy patches all over them. It was also Alex's birthday and the new eleven-year-old had asked for money as a present, so Kelly took him into the nearest market town and opened a bank account for him.

Perignac was bustling with people. Kelly and Alex were standing in a cheese queue when someone she vaguely recognised hailed them.

'*Madame Taylor, bonjour!* What a happy coincidence!'

Kelly stared at him blankly, then

suddenly remembered. He was the other shepherd in the valley and a close friend of Jean-Paul's.

'Oh, goodness, yes — *Monsieur . . . ?*

He pumped her hand up and down. 'Gerard. Gilbert Gerard.' He beamed down at Alex and shook his hand, too. '*Alors! Bon anniversaire, petit!*'

'How do you know it's my birthday?' Alex was amazed.

'Well, my friend Jean-Paul told me. And he sent you a message.'

'Oh?' Alex was suddenly quiet and he was trying to pretend not to be too interested, but his eyes were big and round. 'For me?'

He glanced up at Kelly as if checking to see if she was disappointed that the message wasn't for her. She was, but she daren't show it, and kept her smile rigidly in place.

'Yes. It is in this box,' Monsieur Gerard indicated the cardboard box he was carrying, all tied up with string. 'He could not come down from the mountain to get it himself, so he asked me to do it for him.'

'Well, Alex, aren't you going to see what it is Jean-Paul's sent you?' Kelly prompted when she saw how reluctant Alex was to take the box.

'You open it,' Alex said sulkily and stuck his hands in his pockets.

'Oh, dear! That's not very polite.'

She smiled ruefully up at Gilbert Gerard's puzzled face as she bent to undo the string around the box, guessing immediately what she was going to find inside. She was right.

'Oh, Alex! Look! Isn't he adorable!'

Kelly picked up the tiny black and white puppy and cuddled it against her. It mewed like a kitten and licked her chin. Alex gave it one cursory glance and twisted his face.

'It's all right,' he said, scuffing his shoe.

'*Eh, bien!*' The shepherd nodded amiably. 'I must go. It was lucky meeting you here. I was just about to drive to Labadette with the little dog. If you don't want him, I can take him back . . . ?'

'Oh, no!' Kelly hugged the puppy more tightly to her and it gave a tiny yap. 'No, he's lovely. We'll keep him, won't we, Alex?'

But Alex had wandered off.

'I apologise for my son, Monsieur Gerard. Please tell Jean-Paul that — well, say thank you, will you, and . . . ' Kelly wanted to ply him with questions, but how could she without seeming too obvious? 'How is he? Have you seen him? Is he well?'

The words came tumbling out. In her embarrassment she buried her face in the soft black and white furry ball she was holding.

'*Alors!*' The man waved a hand in the air. 'You know Jean-Paul. He does not say much. Did you not see him when he came down from the mountain last week?'

'He came down from the mountain?'

'Yes! A man cannot survive up there on nothing but fresh air. He came down for supplies. We take turns. This week it is my turn. You did not see him?'

He was frowning, surprised that Jean-Paul hadn't made his presence known.

'No.' She smiled weakly and shook her head. 'No. I suppose he was too busy. Would you — would you please tell him that . . . '

'Yes, *madame*?'

What could she say? Tell Jean-Paul that it was unforgivable of him not to have called to see her? Tell him she was crazy about him and couldn't wait for him to get back? Ask him to please, please make contact with her in order to clarify just exactly where they stood?

'Oh, nothing. Just tell him I said hello — and Alex says thank you.'

The man glanced at the hunched shoulders of the boy and his eyes narrowed. Then he smiled, touched a finger to his forehead and sauntered off among the busy market stalls.

★   ★   ★

'I just don't understand you, Alex Taylor!' Kelly scolded when they were

228

safely in the car and heading back to Labadette. 'That was so rude!'

'I don't want a present from Jean-Paul.'

'Alex! You've wanted a dog for as long as I can remember, and Jean-Paul has been kind enough to give you one. I think a little bit of gratitude is called for, don't you?'

'I don't want the dog. You keep it. It's probably for you anyway.'

So that was it. He still felt jealous about losing Jean-Paul to her.

'Well, if you really don't want him, then I'd love him.' She glanced in the rear-view mirror, expecting to see the puppy climbing all over the seat, but all was quiet back there. 'What shall we call him?'

'I don't care. You decide.'

Kelly tried to keep her irritation from showing.

Later that night, after Alex had gone to bed and the puppy, who still had no name, was curled up on a cushion in the corner of the old settee, Kelly decided to phone Sylvie.

'So, how's the clan?' she asked as Sylvie picked up.

'What's wrong?' her sister asked immediately.

'Why should anything be wrong?'

'It's your tone of voice. Too bright by far. Not bright like, 'Hey, isn't life wonderful!' but bright like, 'Hey, I feel miserable but I'm doing my best to sound happy'.'

Kelly really didn't appreciate being sussed out so rapidly.

'Look, can we just talk and slip gradually into what's bothering me?'

'Sure. Alex OK?'

'He's going through a difficult phase.'

'I'm not surprised. His father's run off with somebody who should be his grandmother and his mother's got the hots for the local shepherd. How is the good shepherd, by the way?'

It all came tumbling out. The fact that she didn't know where she stood. Peter was back in England, crying on Maggie's shoulder. Jean-Paul was keeping his distance and Alex was acting like she'd stolen his one and only friend from him. And he wouldn't even look at the cute little dog Jean-Paul had sent him for his birthday.

'By the way, thank you for sending those books for Alex,' she added, remembering the parcel that had arrived two days ago. 'Did he ring you? He said he would, but he won't do anything when I'm around these days.'

'Don't worry. He rang. We had quite a long chat.'

'Really? He hardly speaks to me at the moment.'

'He'll get over it. Just give him time.'

'But, Sylvie, my son was the light of my life. He was my little Prince Charming. But suddenly he's turned into a gremlin.'

'Well, that's because you took his Prince Charming away from him. He figures Jean-Paul is his property and he can't imagine why he should prefer to spend time with you.'

'That's all very well, but Jean-Paul is *not* spending time with me. I haven't seen him for ages. No messages. Nothing. I'm drowning in confusion and misery and I don't know what to do about it.'

'Sit tight and wait. Something will turn up. Just go with the flow. What else can you do?'

'Nothing, I suppose, short of going up the mountain and dragging him away from his blooming sheep.'

'If you think he's worth it, yes. By the way, I gather Alex quite likes the idea of boarding-school after all.'

'He what?' Kelly cried down the phone.

'He hasn't mentioned it?'

'No, of course he hasn't mentioned it. I'm only his mother, after all.'

'Apparently he's talked it over with Peter. Sorry, Kelly. I thought you would know all about it.'

Kelly swallowed dryly. 'Oh, God, Sylvie, my life is in ruins,' she said desolately.

'Don't talk rot! Anyway, the only thing to do with ruins is to pick up the pieces and start re-building.'

Kelly gritted her teeth and felt ashamed of her moment of weakness.

'You don't know a good name for a black and white puppy, do you?' she asked in a croaky voice.

'What happened? Did you win him in a raffle or something?'

'Oh, Sylvie! Thank you!'

'What for?'

'Well, he is a bit of a bonus in my life at the moment. I'll call him Raffles.'

'You always were a sucker for dogs. That's why I couldn't understand why you married Peter — dog-hater number one in the world.'

'His new woman's got two hulking great red setters.'

'You're joking! He won't last five minutes with her. You'd better look out — he'll be trying to inveigle his way back into your bed before you can say Jack Robinson.'

'He already has. But I sorted him out good and proper.'

'What did you do? Send him packing?'

'No. Actually, I slept in the bath!'

'What are you going to do now?'

'I'm going to wake Alex and give him a piece of my mind — but gently.'

* * *

Alex wasn't asleep when she tapped on his door. He was propped up in bed, knees drawn up, reading his latest Harry Potter for the sixth time.

'I want a word with you,' she ground out, trying to remember to keep a half-smile on her face, just to fool him.

'What about?' He continued reading, or pretending to.

'About life, young man. You may only be eleven years old, but it's time you understood a few things.'

The book dropped from his hands like a lead weight. He drew himself up and retreated further into his pillows.

'I've just been speaking to your Aunt Sylvie and it seems you've told her something you thought I might not be interested in. That you *want* to go to boarding-school?'

'Oh, that,' he said dully.

'So, tell me about it. But first, I want you to know that whatever you decide is all right by me. And if it's your decision, you can't blame me or your father or anybody else if it goes wrong. Right?'

'Yes, I suppose so.'

'There's no 'suppose so' about it, Alex. That's the way it is in the adult world and you might as well start learning all about it right now.

But where should she start?

'Men and women, Alex, go together like bread and peanut butter, only sometimes it doesn't work out. Just like when you make a new friend and think he or she's wonderful, then you find they're not so wonderful after all. What do you do? You say cheerio.

'That's what happened between your father and me, only it's a bit more serious, because we were married and we had you. But the fact that we're separated now doesn't mean that you're not still our son.

'And because men and women don't like living alone, especially when they're young — well, youngish — they partner up with somebody else. And if they're lucky and it works out, they might live happily ever after. Like you and Guillaume maybe.'

She stopped to take a deep breath and Alex's mournful eyes stared at her.

'I've fallen out with Guillaume,' he said.

'OK, so not like you and Guillaume. You and Guillaume are getting a divorce and soon you'll both find new friends and partners and everything will be fine again. Do you see what I'm getting at, Alex?'

'You're talking about you and Jean-Paul, aren't you?'

'Maybe. Right now, I have no idea where I'm going, but I'm not going back to a life with your father. You never got on with your father, anyway. Well, did you?'

He pulled in his mouth and shook his head vigorously. 'No.'

'Well then?'

There was a thud and a startled yelp from downstairs. Kelly went to the door and hovered momentarily.

'I'd better go and see what Raffles is up to. He's probably fallen off the settee.'

'Raffles?'

'Your dog. I had to call him something. You can change it if you want, but he needs a name he can get used to soon.'

'Raffles is OK. Anyway, they won't let me take him to boarding-school, will they?'

'No. Do you still want to go?'

He gnawed on his bottom lip as if it was a piece of raw meat.

'I think so. If I go, can I come back here in the holidays?'

'Of course!'

'And visit Maggie when her grand-children are there?'

'If you want — and if it's all right with Maggie.'

'In that case, I'd like to go.'

The wind was being knocked right out of her sails, but she had to go with it. Go with the flow, Sylvie had said.

★ ★ ★

By October, Raffles had grown into a respectable, half-sized border collie with short, sturdy legs and a white feathery tail to be proud of. Alex had almost been won over by the time he went off to his first te.. at boarding-school in Kent.

Kelly was more thai glad to have Raffles for company. The dog stayed close by her at all times and seemed to hang on her every word. Already he was responding favourably to commands.

As the days grew shorter and cooler, Kelly waited with bated breath for the sound of jingling sheep bells in the valley. Then, one grey, damp and misty morning, two things happened to stir the adrenalin and set her pulses racing.

The mail brought the usual bumph, publicity leaflets, the book of the month from the book club she had joined, a new set of CDs, and a hastily-scribbled note from Alex, in which he told her he was enjoying himself. There was also a very positive response from an art agent.

And the village was alive with the news that the *transhumance* had started. The sheep were already on the middle plateau. After resting and grazing for a few days they would return to the valley and their winter quarters. And she would see Jean-Paul again.

Kelly felt suddenly breathless. She couldn't believe she had managed to survive three whole months without him, living only on the memory of those fleeting but magical times with him.

First, she telephoned the agent. This was a major breakthrough. It was work and she would be paid for it. She had enjoyed some minor successes years ago before marrying Peter. Now, she didn't have a husband and baby to tie her down any more. The offer of work couldn't have come at a better time, since the pennies in the coffers were getting decidedly few.

The agent was a charming man with a soft, Scottish lilt.

'Well then, Kelly, if you could just hop on the next plane to London to meet the publishers and sign the contract . . . '

'Oh — does it have to be so soon? I mean, couldn't it wait until next week or — or the week after, preferably?' She knew she was risking losing the contract to someone more readily available, but she had to ask. How could she possibly not be here when Jean-Paul arrived?

'My dear,' the agent said quietly but firmly, 'it's essential that we get things sewn up right away. It won't take long, I promise you. A quick hop over the Channel, contracts over lunch, and you could be back home again within twenty-four hours.'

'Oh, well, if it's going to be that quick . . . '

All she had to do, as the agent said, was hop on a plane to London, sign a contract and rush back. She might even fit in a brief visit to see Alex and still be back in good time to welcome Jean-Paul with open arms. At least the trip would keep her mind occupied so that the time wouldn't drag so much. The last few weeks had been agony.

She booked her flight, confirmed all the arrangements with the agent, then phoned Peter. It was half-term, which meant that Alex would be with him, probably staying with Maggie up in Norfolk. That had been the arrangement. Half-terms with Peter — that was about as much as he could stand, and as much as Alex would give him; and the bigger holidays of Easter, summer and Christmas with Kelly. At least, she hoped he would want to spend Christmas with her, but the pull to be at Maggie's with her grandchildren was going to be strong competition.

Peter sounded stressed. She noticed it the minute he answered the phone.

'Have I called at a bad time?' she said.

'Is there any other kind? It's chaos here. I've got half the staff down with a virus and some suspicious anomalies on a new account. And at the moment it looks like it's my fault. The boss was shouting blue murder at me this morning and threatening a none-too-golden handshake if I don't put matters right. So, what did you call for?'

'I'm going to be in London tomorrow and the next day. I thought if you were staying at Maggie's with Alex I could use the flat.'

'What are you coming to London for?'

'It looks like I've found myself a job. It's only a fleeting visit to sign a contract, but I couldn't come to England and not see Alex. I thought we might all meet on Saturday for lunch somewhere.'

'Yes — yes, all right. I'll leave a key with the porter. Don't mind the mess. My cleaning lady quit on me. Give me a ring when you arrive, OK?'

She hung up, wishing that Alex was

old enough to travel through London on his own. She was looking forward to seeing him, but the thought of sharing their time together with Peter, especially when he was in a black mood, was hardly a joyful one.

She packed a bag, then went to bed early since she would be up at the crack of dawn the next morning. She had arranged to drop Raffles off with Remi and then make her way to the airport. As she lay in bed, willing sleep, her eyes drifted to the two carved wooden plaques and her heart fluttered. In a very short time, he would be back in the valley and she would know whether or not her dreams were all in vain. Soon, Jean-Paul, she thought. Soon.

★   ★   ★

Peter had been right about the flat. It *was* a mess. It reminded her of his student's room on the university campus. She half expected to find a supply of empty beer cans and half-eaten mouldy sandwiches under the bed. Oddly enough Peter, who was meticulous in everything he did, was also very untidy. Judging by the state of things his cleaning lady had left some time ago.

Just as she was poking around in cupboards, searching for clean bed-linen, the phone rang. It was Peter.

'Just checking to see if you'd arrived,' he said, sounding much calmer today, though not exactly exhilarated. 'How did it go — the interview or whatever?'

'Very well. They were all extremely friendly, apart from one rather officious type, but I don't have to worry about her. I'll be working from home.'

'What will you be working on?'

'It's a series of children's books. I think it'll be fun and they're paying me well so I'll be able to afford a new roof.'

'Well, you always wanted to do that kind of thing, didn't you?'

'Yes — well . . . ' Kelly didn't want to get embroiled in the subject of what she had wanted to do in the past. It would only lead to the fact that he had always stood in her way and they would end up arguing.

'Is lunch still on tomorrow?' she asked. 'I have a late afternoon flight booked, so if we could eat somewhere near the airport that would be a help. Is that OK?'

'I suppose so.'

'Are you all right, Peter?' You couldn't live twelve years with a man and not know when something was wrong.

'I'm fine. I'm just too tired to think at the moment. Look, I've got to go, I'm working at home on that dicey account and I still haven't found the missing money. We'll pick you up at the flat tomorrow at half-eleven.'

It was a moment or two before Kelly realised that he had hung up.

★   ★   ★

Kelly had some misgivings about seeing Alex. She was sure that he still felt a bit hostile towards her. His letters were frequent and friendly enough, but they were usually too short to give anything away about how he really felt.

However, she needn't have worried. When he saw her he beamed all over his face and rushed to give her a big hug.

'I didn't know you were coming!' he told her.

'There wasn't time, it all happened so quickly.'

'Dad says you've got a job. Does that mean you'll be coming back to England?'

Oh, no! If he had his heart set on her being back in London he was in for a big disappointment.

'No, Alex, I'll be working from France.'

'Oh. OK — great! That means I'll still be able to come over for the holidays. What have you done with Raffles?'

'Remi's looking after him. It's just for two days.'

She looked beyond Alex now to where Peter was standing, leaning against the doorframe like a stranger in his own flat. He was jingling his car keys and looked a bit grey and frazzled.

'Hello, Peter,' she said. 'Pardon my saying so, but you look like something the cat dragged in.'

'I feel it,' he said, pulling at his collar, easing it away from his neck. 'I've been working flat out for about ten days. Are you ready? Shall we go? I've booked us a table at a small restaurant just outside of Stansted.'

'Yes, all right.' Kelly picked up her bags, and noticed that he didn't offer to carry them for her. 'Is Maggie waiting in the car?'

Peter was moving off rapidly ahead, so he probably didn't even hear her question. She looked at Alex and raised her eyebrows.

'Maggie didn't come,' Alex said, wrinkling his nose. 'They had a row.'

'Oh, dear! That's a pity. I was looking forward to seeing her again.'

'Do you like her?'

'Yes, as a matter of fact I do.'

'She likes you too. She told me so.'

'Well, I won't ask what the row was about.'

'It was about nothing, as usual. Dad's spitting mad most of the time. I'm looking forward to going back to school.'

'Do you really like it at boarding-school, Alex?' She held her breath, hoping she wasn't unearthing a Pandora's box of miseries.

'It's great,' he said with genuine enthusiasm. 'They've got a home farm and I get to help with the animals. It's not the same as having animals of your own, but it's better than not having them at all.'

Peter was already sitting behind the wheel of his car with the engine running. Kelly sat next to him while Alex piled into the back seat. She shivered as she got in, glad that the heating was on full blast. It had turned cold and there was a misty rain falling.

'Maggie sends apologies, but she thinks she's coming down with something,' Peter muttered.

'Oh, I see.' Kelly glanced behind and caught Alex's eye. She winked and he gave her a lop-sided grin in return.

The roads were busy with nose-to-tail traffic, the surfaces black and greasy. Peter was a good driver, but he was also an impatient one, constantly berating the other motorists.

'Moron!' he yelled out as he finally got around a driver who had been taking his time in the fast lane. 'They shouldn't be in this lane driving like dithering old women.'

He put his foot down and zoomed off, one hand a fist in the air as he shouted at the other driver. Kelly held her breath and braced her feet, feeling suddenly very nervous. He was already passing the speed limit and her heart was jumping into her mouth as he blasted people out of the way.

'Peter! Slow down! We're not in that much of a hurry!' she protested.

'For Pete's sake, don't you start! You sound just like Maggie. And stop doing that,' he added, seeing her foot pressing an imaginary brake pedal. 'You haven't got a brake on your side.'

'Dad!' Alex only got one word out and Peter rounded on him, actually turning in his seat, his face going from grey to purple.

'Shut up, Alex!'

That's when it happened. He gave a shudder and cried out in pain. His hands left the steering wheel and before Kelly could do anything about it, the car had spun out of control. There was a discord of blasting horns and screeching brakes. She heard Alex scream — 'Mum!' and the car was rolling, turning over and over, and her seat-belt was cutting her in half.

The sound of scraping metal was deafening as the car skidded on its roof. She hung there, suspended helplessly, pain searing through her, watching showers of sparks pass her by. Then everything went black.

Such A Tragedy

A curtain of rain poured down over the edge of the big black umbrella that Robert held over Kelly and Alex. For a moment everything went fuzzy and unreal and she felt as if it was just a bad dream, or that she was watching a film and any moment now the list of players would slide up the darkened screen and the ads would come on.

But everything continued grey and wet and cold and people passed by her with mournful faces, and spoke soothing, sympathetic words that echoed slightly and were as blurred as her vision.

They had told her she shouldn't attend the funeral. It was too soon after the accident. There was a heavy dressing on her forehead which had been split open and stitched up, and her right arm was in a sling with more stitches holding together the long lacerations caused by a piece of torn metal.

They'd had to be cut out of the car. She remembered none of it, which was just as well. Peter, they told her, was already dead when the police arrived on the scene. They found out later that it wasn't the crash that had killed him, but a massive heart attack.

Alex was miraculously unhurt, apart from a minor burn on his collar bone, caused by the friction of his seat-belt. For that she was more than thankful, though he had been terribly traumatised and the doctors told her it would be some time before he came out of it. The fact that he had distracted his father seconds before the crash had embedded itself in his mind. He blamed himself for everything.

'Are you ready to go, Kelly?' Robert said gently and she smiled and nodded.

She started to walk with him back to the car, then saw the lonely figure of Maggie standing on the other side of

Peter's grave. She was still elegant, but today she looked her age and her eyes were brimming with tears.

'Just a minute,' Kelly said. 'I must say goodbye to Maggie.'

Alex didn't go with her, but went with Sylvie and the children, back down the cemetery path where the cars were waiting.

'Are you going to be all right, Maggie?' Kelly asked when she got close enough to speak without raising her voice.

Maggie dabbed at her eyes and blew her nose, then she gave a trembling smile and nodded.

'Yes, my dear. How about you?'

Kelly looked away, looked at the freshly-made-up grave covered with masses of flowers. Part of her life was lying buried under them. It hadn't been a wonderful life, but it hadn't been all bad either. There had been good times — in the early days — when they had both tried so hard to make it work.

'I'm fine. I'm just worried about

Alex. Oh, Maggie, how can I make him see that Peter didn't die because of him?'

'He needs time. And a lot of tender, loving care.'

Kelly drew in a deep breath. 'Yes, I'm sure you're right.'

'We'll keep in touch, I hope?'

'Of course.' Maggie had been so kind, despite her own grief over the loss of Peter. 'Well, I'd better go. Thank you, Maggie, for everything.'

★   ★   ★

By the time they reached Pau, Kelly was beginning to feel much better. She still ached from head to toe, but at least it was bearable now, and the painkillers the hospital had given her were just strong enough to allow her to drive, with care, without making her drowsy.

Alex was awfully quiet. He hadn't uttered a word since they left London.

'Think you can navigate for me?' she asked him, making doubly sure his seat-belt was fastened.

He nodded and stared down at the map she passed over to him. She had already marked out the route with an iridescent yellow marker pen.

'You can talk to me, you know, Alex. I'm not going to bite your head off.'

'Yes, I know.'

She smiled and stroked his head, surprised at how easily the lump in her throat kept returning when she thought how close she had been to losing him. They had both been so terribly lucky.

'Fine. Let's go, shall we? Easy does it, eh?'

It was painful, driving, but she had been determined to get back to Labadette. Jean-Paul must have been back in the valley at least a week and be worrying about her.

She had to make several stops to rest. Her nerves were still bothering her, on top of the pain, and she was driving badly because of it. The last thing she wanted was another accident.

'Are you all right, Mum?' Alex asked

as she pulled off the road into a picnic site and sat for a few moments with her head resting on the steering wheel because the hammer inside there seemed to be striking steel.

'Don't worry, Alex. I'll get us home safe and sound. Only another three quarters of an hour and we should be in our valley. And then maybe I'll sleep for a week — well, a few hours anyway. How about you?'

'I'm all right.' Alex blinked straight ahead and nibbled on a thumbnail. 'Have you told Jean-Paul about it? The accident.'

Kelly sighed. 'I think he knows, but I'm not certain. The hospital wrote straight away.'

It had been difficult contacting the village. She hadn't thought to carry any telephone numbers. Old Remi didn't have a telephone and Jean-Paul wouldn't be there anyway. A nurse who spoke some French had kindly offered to write a letter for her, seeing that she was incapacitated. She could only assume that he had received the news by now that they were all right.

It was already dusk by the time Kelly parked the car outside the old French house that was now her home. As she got out stiffly, moving with great care, she glanced up at Jean-Paul's cottage. It was all shuttered up and there was no sign of light anywhere.

'He isn't home,' Alex said. 'Maybe he's down at the café.'

'Maybe.' A great tiredness had come over her now that she didn't have to push herself onwards. 'We'll just leave a light on the veranda. He'll see it when he comes back and know we're here.'

As she passed through the door into the hall a slight breeze caught the chimes hanging above her head. It made the hairs on the back of her neck rise eerily. It should have been a warm, welcoming sound, but it somehow emphasised the emptiness of the place.

A damp chill descended on her as she wandered into the living-room and sank down wearily on the settee. Her head was still thudding and she felt as if her veins were full of lead.

'I could light the stove,' Alex suggested tentatively.

'Think you could?' She looked at him from beneath drooping eyelids, thinking that it would be a miracle if she was ever able to move again. 'That would be wonderful, Alex.'

As if he had been born to it, Alex had the stove going within minutes and was boiling the kettle for a cup of tea. Kelly was proud of him. He still wasn't looking at her properly — more out of the corner of his eye and fleeting glances thrown over his shoulder — but that didn't matter. Words were at last coming out of his mouth and he was doing things. The rest would come later. If it didn't, he wasn't her son.

★ ★ ★

Jean-Paul did not come that night and there was still no sign of him the next day. Kelly was suffering the after-effects

258

of delayed shock and fatigue and having trouble getting her body motivated. Everything hurt and she had to keep sitting down.

'Why don't you go down to the village and see your friends, Alex?' she suggested, seeing how restless the boy was.

They were sitting on the veranda in the warm October sunshine. In England there were gales and reports of heavy snow showers with temperatures dropping overnight to below zero. She was glad they weren't still over there. Sylvie had asked them to stay with her for a few days, but with four children and another on the way, it would have been an imposition. Besides, Kelly had been anxious to get back home to France.

'Well?' She looked at her son who was sitting on the edge of the veranda, his legs swinging over the end. He hadn't answered her, but went on staring out at the distant mountain peaks that were once more getting their snowy caps on ready for winter. 'Go on,

Alex. It'll do you good. Look, if you're frightened to leave me on my own, forget it,' Kelly said. 'I'm all right, really I am.'

His eyes touched her and flashed away again in a quick burst of blue that matched the sky.

'It's not that.'

'Then what is it?'

She saw the vestige of a tiny shrug, then silence reigned once more.

After a long time, Alex said, almost to himself, 'Why doesn't he come?'

Kelly felt the hairs prickle again on her legs and arms. The same thought had been going through her head. Why didn't Jean-Paul come?

'I don't know. He must be busy somewhere. The sheep . . . '

'The sheep are in the winter pasture, but he's not with them.'

Kelly sat up straight and swallowed hard. 'How do you know that?'

'I went over there and looked this morning. You were still asleep.'

'But where are they?' She had

thought she heard the distant tinkle of bells earlier in the day, but there were no sheep dotted about the hillsides and she thought the wind must be carrying the sound from the next valley.

'Just over the ridge — over there.' He pointed with his chin.

'But they can't be Jean-Paul's sheep. He would be with them.'

'They are his sheep. I took my binoculars. Jean-Paul wasn't there. It was old Remi looking after them. Tricot was there too. They didn't see me.'

Kelly felt a sudden rise of panic fluttering beneath her ribcage, threatening to choke her.

'Did you see Raffles? He's quite big now.'

Alex shook his head. 'There was just Tricot.'

'I've got to go and talk to Remi.'

She stood up quickly, too quickly, and it made the earth tilt dangerously. She reached out and grabbed the veranda post for support. Her knees started to buckle and her mouth went dry and cold.

'Mum!'

'I'm all right, Alex,' she gasped, sinking back down again on the seat and closing her eyes, willing the dizziness to pass. And suddenly her son was throwing himself into her arms, kneeling before her, burying his head against her stomach and weeping bitterly.

'I'm sorry, Mum! I'm sorry!'

Her hands found his head and stroked it. 'Goodness, Alex, what have you got to be sorry for? You didn't do anything wrong.'

'Yes I did! I made Dad angry and it made him have an accident and if I hadn't shouted at him he would still be alive and . . . and you wouldn't be hurt and . . . and so unhappy!'

She leaned forward and dragged him up on to the swing seat beside her.

'Oh, Alex, sweetheart! The accident had absolutely nothing to do with you. I thought you understood — the heart attack — your father would have had that anyway. He could have been at the office, on the Tube, at home with Maggie — anywhere. He was going to have that heart attack, no matter what. That's what killed him. The fact that he was driving at the time and we were with him — well, that made it a lot worse. Not for him, but for us, because we got hurt too. Thank God we were the only ones.'

Alex continued to sob, but his tears were flowing only in small spurts now rather than great rivers.

'I thought — I thought I was being punished for not — for not loving him.'

'Oh, my poor darling.' Kelly pulled him roughly into her arms and hugged him tightly. 'Nobody can punish you for that — only yourself. It's no sin not to love somebody, you know. You mustn't feel guilty.'

'But he was my *father!*'

'Yes, he was your father, Alex, but he wasn't an easy man to love.'

'You loved him, didn't you? You cried when he left home.'

How could she answer that? She had

never been able to understand why she had cried so much after Peter had gone from her life. Maybe it was because she had suddenly found herself in some kind of void, dumped at a complicated crossroads where there were no signs to tell her which way to go. Maybe she felt guilty. Or relieved. Maybe it was a composite of all three and a few other things thrown in for good measure.

'I did love him once, Alex,' she said carefully, measuring every word. 'But love's a funny thing. It can deceive you. I tried very hard to go on loving your father, but — it just didn't work. However, he gave me one precious gift that will always make me grateful. He gave me you, Alex — and I'll always love you, no matter what.'

There was a loud sniff and then he was smiling broadly at her through globules of glycerine tears.

'Maybe Jean-Paul's on holiday,' he said out of the blue.

'Somehow I don't think shepherds take holidays,' she said with a grimace

264

back at him. 'Is it far to the pasture where the sheep are?'

'Not that far. Shall I go and see Remi for you?'

Kelly took a deep breath and shook her head. 'No, we'll go together.'

She stood up tentatively. The giddiness had passed, but she still felt fairly shaky.

★   ★   ★

Remi saw their approach. He stood staring, his hand shading his eyes from the glare of the low evening sun. As they got closer, Kelly could see that his creased old face was marked with astonishment and disbelief.

There was an excited barking as Tricot got their scent and bounded up the hill to meet them. Alex threw his arms about the dog's thick neck and got his face washed by the dog's long, pink tongue, then the pair of them started running together back down to Remi and the sheep.

Kelly followed more slowly, not understanding the expression on the old shepherd's face and the fact that he kept shaking his head as she got closer.

'*Bonsoir*, Remi! Did you not expect to see me back again?'

'Madame Taylor! Is it you? It is really you? And the boy?'

She walked right up to him and he was still scrutinising her face. He grabbed her outstretched hand and squeezed it hard.

'Remi? What is it? Oh, you're looking at this?' Her fingers touched the dressing on her forehead. 'Didn't you know? I sent — or at least, the hospital sent a message to Jean-Paul, but there was no reply. Where is he?'

Remi's head was still going from side to side, his eyes full of wonder. 'You are not dead! Madame Taylor, *you are alive!*'

He staggered to a collection of rocks a few feet away and sat down heavily on one of them, patting at his chest and breathing heavily. She joined him, her legs feeling weak again from the walk.

'Did you think I was dead?' She felt the blood drain from her cheeks.

He nodded slowly. 'We all thought — that letter — it was in such bad French. It spoke of you and a fatal accident . . . '

The hospital had so kindly sent the letter for her when she was barely conscious. She hadn't checked the wording before they sent it. It had seemed impossible to get the details wrong.

'Oh, Remi! Did Jean-Paul think I — I had been killed?'

'But of course! We all did.'

'Oh, no!' Kelly clapped a hand to her mouth as she thought of the shock the news must have been to Jean-Paul.

'*Le pauvre!* It is the first time I have ever seen Jean-Paul drunk. He has been like a crazy man ever since. He does not go to the village. He does not speak, even to me, his oldest friend.'

'Where is he, Remi?' Kelly asked urgently. 'Please tell me where he is.'

Remi gave a long, low whistle. 'You will not find him on your own. He is somewhere up on his mountain. He roams about like a mad bear. I tried to make him come down, but he would not listen to me.'

'I've got to go to him, Remi!'

The old shepherd scraped a gnarled hand over his grizzled jowls and gave her a thoughtful look.

'He will not be on the high mountain. It is late — too dangerous. He will be on the *pont*. The boy will know how to find it. Remember how Alex spent time with Jean-Paul? That is where they went.'

'The plateau! I've been there,' Kelly said with a hopeful smile, remembering the day she had first realised that Jean-Paul wanted her, and she him.

'Alex!' She called the boy to her. 'Alex, Jean-Paul is up on the plateau. Can you remember how to get there?'

'I think so.'

'Good. Come on, I want you to take me up there. We've got to find him as soon as possible.'

'No!' Remi was struggling to get to his feet and having bother sorting out his stiff, arthritic legs. 'It's too late tonight and you are not fit.'

'He's right, Mum!' Alex jumped in wisely. 'It'll be dark soon and you know I can't see in the dark. We'd only get lost.'

Kelly couldn't argue with that. Her desperation to see Jean-Paul again, to put his mind at rest, was making her neurotic. She could understand the pain he must be feeling right now, if he truly loved her. And she was sure now that he did.

'Remi . . . ' She turned to the shepherd. 'Remi, Jean-Paul won't do anything — stupid — will he?'

The old man looked at her, his head to one side, his wrinkled eyes screwed up against the fading light.

'Jean-Paul is the strongest man I know, but this pain he feels is more than he can bear. You came and touched his heart, Madame Taylor. He did not know it for a long time. He even fought against it. I know, believe me. Do anything stupid? I don't think so, but . . . who knows?' He gave a Gallic shrug. 'You must go to him tomorrow, *hein?*'

'Mon Amour...'

Kelly didn't think she would be able to close her eyes that night, but after tossing and turning and staring wide-eyed into the darkness, she eventually drifted off into a deep, dreamless sleep.

She had left the shutters open so that she would wake with the first of the morning light. She didn't want to waste any time in getting to the plateau.

Alex was already up and dressed when she got downstairs. His clothes were so crumpled it looked as if he had slept in them, but she didn't care. Her only priority that day was to find Jean-Paul.

'Are you all right, Mum?' His eyes were full of concern as they scoured her face.

'I'm fine!' she assured him, more confidently than she felt.

The mountains were shrouded in

mist and dark clouds were looming on the horizon. There was a small patch of blue sky above, but even that looked in imminent danger of being swallowed up very soon. Even as she stepped out on to the veranda, splotches of rain were beginning to fall.

Great, she thought. That's all we need.

It was relatively easy going at first. When the day darkened, however, and the rain started falling in sheets, she had to pray that Alex's sense of direction would not fail him.

He strode on ahead, stopping frequently to allow her to catch up. Normally she could have made it easily. However, it was too soon after the accident and she had a long way to go before she recovered her strength. She was certainly making heavy weather of the steep climb, and her feet were beginning to slip and slide on the mud and gravel as the rain pounded it, turning it to mush.

Feeling cold rivulets of rain penetrating around the neck of her waterproof, she veered off towards a clump of trees and sat down on a sawn-off tree bole.

'I'm sorry, Alex,' she called out to him breathlessly. 'I have to rest. Are you sure we're on the right track?'

He came to join her, peering at her through his rain-spattered glasses.

'This is definitely the way, Mum . . .' he said, wiping the back of his hand across his dripping nose and chin. 'I think.'

'Come on,' Kelly sighed, trying not to show her anxiety. 'Let's go on a bit farther.'

Alex was looking worried, but he wasn't about to admit defeat. As their feet squished and slurped in the bog-mossy earth or skidded over stony inclines, she saw his eyes dart about desperately, willing something familiar to emerge.

After another half-hour, Alex came to an abrupt halt.

'I think we're lost,' he said, his lips quivering.

I am not going to panic, Kelly told

273

herself strictly. The weather's bad and I'm lost on a mountain, but it's still broad daylight with hours to go before it gets dark.

The trouble was, she didn't feel as if she could keep going for hours. Her legs were giving out and her shoulder and midriff where the seat-belt had dug into her were hurting like mad.

'Just think positively, Alex,' she said. 'When you used to come up here with Jean-Paul, did you keep going straight up or did you veer off to the left or the right at some point?'

Alex wrinkled his nose and chewed on the side of his mouth.

'I can't remember.'

'Yes, you can. Now, come on — at some stage, didn't Jean-Paul say to you, 'No, Alex, not that way, this way'? And you said to him, 'Oh, yes, I always get that wrong, don't I?''

She wasn't guessing. Somewhere deep down, she had a vague recollection of that very thing happening the day she had come up the mountain with them. The day she had spent the afternoon sketching, and falling in love.

Alex gave a sharp intake of breath and shoved his glasses up his nose. 'Yes! It was funny, because I always went wrong at that spot and Jean-Paul used to laugh at me. I'd go to the left while he went to the right.'

Kelly gave a weak laugh. 'You never did know your left from your right. You definitely take after me in that. Can you remember where it was you went wrong?'

'I think so . . . Oh, no! It was miles back. We should have gone to the right before the tree-line. We went straight on. We'll have to go back.'

Kelly looked about her and pointed off to the right. 'Look, there's a trail there going in the right direction. If we go that way we might come out above where Jean-Paul's plateau is.' Then she had second thoughts. 'Or we might get even more lost. What do you think, Alex?'

Alex stuck his hands into his pockets

and frowned. He frowned for a long time, his mouth working in some mysterious way.

'I've got it!' he yelled and did a little dance, sending up a spray of muddy water and grit.

'Would you care to share it?'

He laughed then. He actually opened his mouth and laughed and nearly choked on the rainwater that deluged him.

'I'd forgotten. Jean-Paul taught me one or two signals — you know, the old whistling language that shepherds use to speak to each other when they're up in the mountains with their sheep.'

'Well, the saints be praised! I hope he taught you a whistle for *au secours*.'

'Not exactly. I can only remember two of the signals.'

'What are they?' She held her breath and hoped they weren't anything to do with 'what foul weather' or 'see you in the pub tonight'.

'The first one is 'where are you?' and it sounds like this — I think.' Alex cupped his hands around his mouth and let out a series of shrill whistles that lifted Kelly's head, but she wasn't sure they would be strong enough to carry across the valley through the wind and the rain.

'What's the other one?'

'Well, the other one's more or less the answer to the first one. It means 'I'm here'.'

'Try it.'

Again a series of whistles, slightly shorter this time, and in a different sequence.

'Come on, Alex. Let's move along this track. The valley looks as if it opens up below us over there. Keep going with those whistles. You never know — Jean-Paul might hear you.'

She didn't hold out much hope, but she couldn't let Alex see that. If all else failed they would just have to try to backtrack. It was either that or sit tight and wait for Remi to organise a search party.

Alex whistled and whistled until he

could produce no more than a feeble bleep. Poor little soul, he was trying so hard, but there was a time to give up and this was it. Kelly gave him a tight hug.

'Never mind,' she said. 'We'll go back . . . '

As she spoke the wind dropped and they both looked up together at the sound of a shrill whistle coming from somewhere quite close.

'It's him!' Alex squeaked. 'It's Jean-Paul! We've found him!'

They almost ran towards the sound, slithering on shale, crashing through shrubs and low-growing trees, down to a parallel track. They skidded to a halt, looking to left and to right and there, coming towards them, was a dark figure, hazy through the mist of driving rain.

'It's not him,' Kelly whispered, heavy with disappointment.

'It is, it is!' Alex shouted and bounded forward.

It wasn't Jean-Paul, but his friend

Gilbert. When he saw them his face registered much the same expression as that of old Remi Dubois.

'*Mon Dieu! Ce n'est pas possible!*'

'We thought you were Jean-Paul!' Alex complained.

Gilbert nodded and scratched his head beneath the great black pancake of a berry he wore.

'I would like to be there to see his face when he sees you two,' he said.

'But, Gilbert,' Kelly said, 'what are you doing on the mountain? I thought all the sheep were down in the valley now.'

'They are. I came to look for Jean-Paul also, to try to persuade him to rejoin the human race. Perhaps you might do a more effective job of it.'

'But where is he?' Alex piped up impatiently. 'We've been looking for him, but we got lost. Everything looks so different in the rain.'

'He's not far, I'm sure. Was that you whistling, young man?'

'Yes, but I'm not very good at it.'

'You're good enough.'

'But Jean-Paul didn't answer.'

'No. He probably thought it was me and he doesn't want to see me.'

'Should I try again?'

Gilbert rubbed his big nose.

'No. I will take you there. Let's surprise him, *hein*?' He looked into Kelly's face and smiled broadly. 'I think it is very important, *non*?'

'Very important, Gilbert,' Kelly said.

'*Putain*, that's a pretty eye you've got there.' He looked from the blue and yellowish green marbling around her eye to the dressing on her head and her hand and gave a low whistle, shaking his fingers. 'Ouf! It looks like you have quite a story to tell to Jean-Paul, *hein*?'

They followed in the shepherd's footsteps as he led them across the valley and gradually down, through another, thicker tree-line. A row of flat stepping stones took them across a wide, fast-flowing stream and over terrain that was lush and green. The rain had finally eased and the sun was struggling through the mist.

Just when Kelly thought she could not go another step, they reached a ridge that overhung the verdant pastures where the sheep were housed in springtime. With cries of delight, Kelly and Alex recognised the small lake where they had picnicked.

'Look!' Gilbert pointed ahead.

But Kelly had already seen the lone figure sitting on a rock, big shoulders hunched, head bowed. A small black and white dog stood patiently beside him, and as they watched, Jean-Paul reached out and fondled the animal's ears.

'Is that Raffles?' Alex asked excitedly.

'Yes,' Kelly replied, a break in her voice. 'That's him.'

'Come on . . . ' Alex started forward, but Gilbert pulled him back and shook his head with a gentle and knowing smile.

'Wait, boy! Jean-Paul has need to see your mother first, I think.' He looked across at Kelly and nodded. 'It is not difficult from here. Alex and I will follow — later.'

Alex looked a little put out, but then he inclined his head and gave her a watery smile. 'Go on, Mum.'

She needed no second telling.

★ ★ ★

Picking her way carefully over the tussocky overgrown track she willed her legs to keep going. At first, the distance between them didn't seem to get any less. Then she was only a few yards away. He still hadn't heard her, but Raffles had. The dog gave an ecstatic yelp and shot towards her. Jean-Paul remained hunched over as he had been all the while she was descending the hill.

Then, from the ridge behind, a staccato string of whistles sallied forth as Gilbert sent a message winging through the air. Jean-Paul's back straightened. He looked over his shoulder and got slowly to his feet, turning to face Kelly, his expression unforgettable in that precious moment that seemed suspended in time.

He emitted a guttural sound that struck her heart and she felt tears well into her eyes as he staggered forward a step or two, still not believing what he was seeing.

Jean-Paul shook his head, looked away, and looked back. She moved closer and saw the glisten of moisture in his gaze.

'Kelly?' It was a croak; he held out his hands and uttered her name again in a hoarse shout. '*Ke-lly!*'

Kelly didn't know how she found the strength to cover the remaining distance between them. She could feel her legs buckling like soft rubber, but they carried her forward until she collapsed, a quaking, sobbing mass in his arms.

He buried his face in her hair. She tasted the salt of their mingled tears. His heart thudded against her as he pulled her tight to him until they were one.

'They said you were dead!' he murmured against her ear. 'A fatal accident. They said that you and the boy died with your husband.'

She clung to him, trying to get a grip on her senses, trying to find enough control to speak without crying hysterically and collapsing in a jelly-like heap at his feet.

'Kelly! My Kelly!' His fingers explored her face; those big, tough fingers that could be so gentle, so loving. 'To begin with, I thought you had gone back to England, back to your husband. They said he was here, that you were living together as man and wife again. I thought — *I have lost her*. She prefers life with this man who can give her the things I cannot give her. I was so miserable, so angry, so sad!'

'Oh, Jean-Paul, no! It wasn't like that. It wasn't like that at all.'

'My love for you is the strongest emotion I have ever felt. I have nothing to give you, Kelly. *Nothing*! Am I crazy to think that you could love me?'

'Ssh!' She pressed her fingers against his mouth to stop the flow of words, but he was determined to have his say. He crushed her fingers in his hand, then kissed them hungrily.

'I was trying to forget you, push you out of my heart, when news of the accident arrived, and I knew that even if you were dead, I could never stop loving you. *Never!*'

The sun was finally breaking through. Kelly could feel its warm caress on her head.

'Jean-Paul, would you just kiss me — please!'

'If I kiss you now I might not be able to stop.'

She smiled. 'I'd like nothing better, but that could be embarrassing. I'm not the only lost sheep who needs taking back to the fold. Alex is back there somewhere with Gilbert.'

'Ah!' He was peering over her shoulder. 'I see them. Already they are too close, but I am going to kiss you anyway because I can't wait any longer.'

He clamped her head between his hands and fell on her mouth, devouring her lips, a low, animal moan rumbling in his throat as his body moulded itself to hers.

Reluctantly she forced herself to draw back, disturbed by the raw longing in his brown eyes.

'Jean-Paul, my husband did die in that crash. Alex feels responsible for the accident. He wasn't, of course. I've tried to explain things to him, but — we have to be gentle with him.'

'Poor little one. Do not worry, Kelly. He will be all right.' He stepped away from her now and held his arms open for Alex. 'Alex, my friend! You are back! I have missed you.'

Alex hesitated, glanced at Kelly, then leapt forward and clung to Jean-Paul, smothering his sobs in the Basque's broad chest. Jean-Paul patted the boy's shoulders and pushed him gently away.

'Hey, Alex!' he said gruffly. 'What do you think of little Raffles, *hein*? I have been training him how to be a sheep-dog like Tricot.'

'Have you? Is he good?'

'Well, he is still young, so he gets a little distracted from time to time, but I think he will grow to be a fine dog.'

He looked up and caught the smiling glance of his friend, Gilbert.

'*Alors!* It was you whistling to me across the valley.'

'No, no! It was Alex. You taught him well.'

'Well done, Alex. I am sorry I did not respond. But what have you in that backpack of yours?'

Alex beamed at him. 'We've got bread and cheese and . . . '

'Well, that's wonderful. Suddenly I feel very hungry.' He slid an arm about Kelly's waist and pulled her close. 'More hungry than I dare say. Shall we all eat something, then we can go home?'

Later, they watched Gilbert gradually disappear in the direction of his own valley. Jean-Paul's hand found Kelly's and squeezed it tightly. They sat so close that there wasn't even space for a chink of light to find its way through between them.

'Kelly.' His voice was low, his eyes dark. 'There is not much future for you as the wife of a shepherd. I cannot promise you riches or . . . '

'Jean-Paul, right now I don't even want to think of the future. We will talk about that one day, but not now. You are wrong, you know, saying you have nothing to give. You've already the most precious gift of all.'

'What is that, *mon amour?*'

'Your love . . . you! For the moment, that's all I want.'

He kissed her cheek, pressed his face against hers and she heard his breath catch in his throat. 'Let's go home.'

Spring Is Here

'Jean-Paul! Jean-Paul!' It was early spring. The valley was full of nodding daffodils, making carpets of yellow that seemed to forge a golden pathway to the snow-laden mountains.

Kelly was running from the house down the hill and across the winter grazing ground. She skirted the paddocks and ran breathlessly into the big shed where Jean-Paul sat on a three-legged stool. He was pressing great rounds of curd into the moulds that gave the cheese its traditional shape and embossed the family emblem on to it. Later, she would help him wrap it in jute bags, ready to be taken to the drier where they would be stored for months to mature.

He looked up from his work, relaxed and smiling. 'What is it? A letter from Alex?'

After Christmas, Alex had decided to return to his boarding-school and he was doing well there. He wrote to them regularly.

'Yes, there's one from him. He says he still wants to take up farming. I don't know whether that's good or bad, but he seems very determined.'

Jean-Paul shrugged, wiped his hands and came to kiss her. As always, when he got this close to her, Kelly's body melted and her stomach took a delicious dive. But today she was too excited, too full of news to get carried away with his caresses. She detached herself from him and waved a wad of letters in front of his nose.

'Well, I can see that you will not settle until you tell me your news, but be quick about it or my cheese will curdle.'

'Well, first of all, Sylvie says that baby Emma is doing well and that her eldest boy is going to go to Alex's school next term. They'll be in the same form, so that's good, isn't it?'

'Next?'

'The publisher liked the work I did on that last book so much that he's offered me a contract for another three children's books and there's a possibility of doing a wild flower book next spring.'

'It will keep you busy and out of mischief.' He grinned and tousled her hair, which was already untidy from her mad race from the house. '*Alors*? There appears to be another letter there. What is it you are hiding from me? You look guilty. What have you been up to?'

Kelly sucked in air and held her breath. This was the moment she had been planning, waiting for, and was now dreading.

'Jean-Paul, I was thinking that your cottage would make the perfect studio — my paintings, your carvings — um — with a showroom. We could convert the barn — you know — for your furniture. You're such a wonderful carpenter as well as a sculptor and . . . '

He was frowning darkly at her and

her heart was already beginning to sink.

'I have no time for that. I have to make a living — here with the sheep — and the cheese. Besides, who will buy such things?'

'Apparently quite a lot of people. I have an appointment for you to go to Biarritz and talk to the owner of an antiques shop there. They are interested in specialising in hand-made furniture. They already know your work, Jean-Paul, and they love it. I know how happy you are when you are working with wood and . . . '

'Stop! Why? Why are you trying to change me?'

She blinked at him. It was the kind of response she had feared, but she was ready for it.

'I'm not. I wouldn't change you for the world. If you're happy being a shepherd and making cheese for the rest of your life, then that's all right with me. Here! Take the letter. Do what you want with it. It doesn't matter. It's your decision. Go on — tear it up.'

She turned and marched back up to the house, feeling his eyes on her rigid back, burning holes in her all the way. That was all right. He would have some time to stew over what she had said. By the time he got back to the house he would have come to a decision. And he knew that whatever that decision was, she would support him.

She really didn't care what he did, as long as they were together and happy. And they were very, very happy. She had never thought it could ever be like this, but Jean-Paul had proved her wrong.

*   *   *

At the supper table a few hours later, Jean-Paul smiled radiantly at her over his plate of *confit de canard* and *pomme de terre dauphin*. It was his favourite dish and she knew exactly what he was going to ask as he sat down to eat.

'Is there English apple pie and cream for dessert?'

'How did you guess?'

'I am *voyant*. Just like you, Kelly, I can see into the future.'

'Oh, really?'

He frowned at the table wine she had put out, re-corked it and put it to one side. Then he went to the cellar and came back wiping the dust and the cobwebs from a bottle of Haut-Brion 95.

'Where are the candles?' he asked, looking at her speculatively.

'You want candles?'

'And flowers. This is a special occasion.'

'The candles,' she said, producing two long milky white candles from the dresser drawer, 'I can provide.' Fetching a box of matches, her eyes sparkled at him as she lit them.

'And I . . . ' He disappeared for a moment and when he returned he produced a posy of wild flowers from behind his back which he must have gathered in near darkness on his way home. ' . . . have the flowers.'

'They're beautiful, Jean-Paul. So, what is this special occasion?' She kissed him and put his posy in a small crystal vase. 'It's nobody's birthday or anniversary that I know of.'

'We have two things to celebrate — well, there are lots of things, but two major things which will affect our lives greatly, my love.'

'Oh?'

'First . . . ' He poured out two glasses of ruby red wine and passed her one. ' . . . I'm not going to sell my sheep or give up making cheese. Not until I have to. I promised my grandfather that I would carry on the family tradition that I am proud of.'

Kelly clicked her glass to his and took a sip of her wine. She was only slightly disappointed and knew it to be purely a selfish reaction, but she wasn't going to show it.

'And the second thing?'

'Oh, I'm not finished with the first yet,' he said, his eyes sparkling. 'It is an idea I have been playing with for some time, and now, I think it is going to be possible.

'I spoke to Gilbert a few days ago and he agrees. We are going to come together and form a cooperative, maybe even take on another shepherd. That will give me time to concentrate on the four loves of my life and still keep my finger on the family cheese business.'

'*Four* loves of your life?' she echoed. 'Jean-Paul, have you been holding out on me?'

His hand shot out across the table and held hers, his thumb stroking her skin, making her whole body tingle and melt. His eyes were like brown velvet, soft and deep.

'Four loves, Kelly. My dream of being a master carpenter, you, Alex and . . .' Here he stopped and his eyes grew warm and misty in the light of the candles.

'And?'

'The second major thing that will soon affect our lives.'

'Which is?'

He took her glass, put it to one side and held both her hands across the table as he gazed into her eyes.

'I think we should get married.'

Kelly's mouth gaped slightly, then she bit down on her lip and her mouth quivered into a smile.

'You do?'

'I do.'

He pulled her hand to his mouth and kissed the palm. She gave an ecstatic shudder and didn't care that the meal on the table between them was growing cold.

He rose and pulled her away from the table. As always, she fitted to him like a glove. He wound his big arms around her and his mouth found hers.

'Jean-Paul, I love you so much!' she murmured against his lips.

'Does that mean yes?'

Her eyes misted with tears of happiness as she gazed at this man she adored.

'Yes,' she said simply. 'Oh, Jean-Paul . . . '

'I know, I know!' he said, lowering his lips to hers. 'I am wonderful. Now, kiss me, my soon-to-be wife!'

The End

Peter's tall, slim silhouette. She had no desire to rush into his arms, but she felt comforted, seeing him there, knowing that he would be in control of the situation.

'It's all right, Kelly,' he said, coming forward and placing a light kiss on her cheek. 'Don't worry. He's back, safe and sound, all in one piece.'

'I'll go and make a pot of tea,' Maggie said, touching Kelly's arm fleetingly as she swept past them into the house.

Peter turned worried eyes on Kelly. 'You didn't mind too much, did you — Maggie collecting you from the airport?'

'No. Actually I like her. She seems very nice.'

Peter had taken a step back and was scrutinising her. He hadn't looked at her like that since their first date.

'You look different. What have you done to yourself?'

She felt a sudden rush of heat to her cheeks. It had never occurred to her that being in love would show itself quite so visibly.

'Nothing!' she said and pushed past him. 'Where's Alex?'

'In the lounge — it's this way.'

Alex was slumped in the corner of a huge leather sofa, swamped by a white towelling bathrobe. He looked as if he had recently been scrubbed clean and his hair was still damp and plastered flat to his head. He also looked tiny and lost in that vast room.

As she entered, his eyes flickered momentarily over her, but he didn't jump up and come flying into her arms as she had expected he would. Tucking his chin well in, he avoided any further eye contact.

'Hello, Alex,' she said cheerily, swallowing back a sobbing cry of relief to see him unharmed and repressing an urge to smother him in a motherly embrace. 'I hear you've been causing problems. That's not like you, sweetheart. Like to talk about it?'

He slid her a look and shook his head